PASSAGES™

MANUSCRIPT
2

ARIN'S JUDGMENT

PAUL MCCUSKER

FROM ADVENTURES IN ODYSSEY®

TYNDALE
Tyndale House Publishers, Inc.
Wheaton, Illinois

ARIN'S JUDGMENT
Copyright © 2005 by Focus on the Family.
All rights reserved. International copyright secured.

ISBN: 1-58997-168-X

Library of Congress has cataloged previous edition as follows:
McCusker, Paul. 1958-
    Arin's judgment / by Paul McCusker.
       p. cm.
    Summary: At the end of World War II, Wade is transported to a war-torn alternate world called Marus, where he finds himself a key figure in a political power struggle and unwittingly helps to bring the Unseen One's judgment on a corrupt people.
    ISBN: 1-56179-774-X
    [1. Space and time Fiction. 2. War Fiction. 3. End of the world Fiction.] I. Title.
    PZ7.M47841635fi   1999
    [Fic]—dc21   99-14247
                                                    CIP

A Focus on the Family book published by
Tyndale House Publishers, Wheaton, Illinois 60189

TYNDALE is a registered trademark of Tyndale House Publishers, Inc.
Tyndale's quill logo is a trademark of Tyndale House Publishers, Inc.

No part of this publication may be reproduced, stored in a retrieval system, or transmitted in any form or by any means—electronic, mechanical, photocopy, recording, or otherwise—without prior permission of the publisher.

The author is represented by the literary agency of Alive Communications, 7680 Goddard Street, Suite 200, Colorado Springs, CO 80920.

Editors: Larry Weeden and Mick Silva
Cover design: Greg Sills
Cover copy: Larrilee Frazier

Printed in the United States of America
2 3 4 5 6 7 8 9 /10 09 08 07 06 05

to John Eldredge,
who tears down, to rebuild with love

Adventures in Odyssey Presents
Passages, Book II

PROLOGUE

❧─────────❧

Jack Allen brought his old, blue Buick to a stop alongside the curb. Jagged ice crunched loudly beneath the tires. It reminded him of the sounds of a child eating a candy cane. Otherwise, the cold, snow-filled day was silent.

"Well," said John Avery Whittaker from the passenger side of the car. "I remember when this part of Odyssey was nothing but open fields and farmland. The town has grown a lot."

Jack looked through the smeared windshield at the avenue of middle-class homes. They were built in a Colonial style popular in the early 1970s. The sun, barely a smudge of white in the overcast sky, gave a hazy look to the bare trees and shrubs that poked like pencil marks out of the snow-covered lawns. A tall "For Sale" sign waved gently to them from the front of Maude McCutcheon's house. She was the reason they were there.

"Do you think we'll find any more manuscripts?" Jack asked as he turned off the car's engine.

Whit, as John Whittaker was best known, smiled. His lips curled up and disappeared under his bushy-white mustache. "I hope so," he said.

Jack pulled a large, brown envelope from the top of the

dashboard. In it was the first clue in a mystery the two men hoped to solve. "Shall we?"

Whit nodded. The two men climbed out of the car and carefully made their way up the icy driveway to the front door of the house. They stepped onto the porch, and Whit rang the doorbell. Somewhere inside, it chimed pleasantly. Jack shivered and withdrew into his overcoat as the wind blew his salt-and-pepper-colored hair in odd directions. Whit's hair, normally wild and disheveled anyway, moved above his head like a white flame. The two men looked at each other and laughed. They'd been friends since childhood and knew what the other was thinking at that moment.

The door was unlocked and opened by a middle-aged man with ruddy cheeks, dark brown hair, and sad eyes. Without a doubt, he was Maude McCutcheon's son. The eyes in particular made it obvious; Whit saw Maude in those eyes.

"Yes?" he asked.

"Hello, Mr. McCutcheon," Jack said. "I'm Jack Allen. I phoned this morning."

"Oh, yes, Mr. Allen. You're the antiques dealer we sold some of my mother's things to."

Jack nodded. "That's right. This is John Avery Whittaker."

"I know Mr. Whittaker," the man said, shaking Whit's hand and smiling. "It's good to see you again."

"It's good to see you, too, Billy."

"How do you two know each other?" Jack asked.

"Billy was a student of mine one year when I taught at the high school. Got an A in English if I remember right."

"Did I?" McCutcheon asked. "It's one of the few A's I got in high school then. Sports took up most of my time. Come in, gentlemen."

The man called Billy led Whit and Jack down a short hallway into the living room. The furniture sat at odd angles, having been pushed aside to leave space for the many packed cardboard boxes. A fire blazed in the fireplace on the far wall. It was the only hint that this room was probably a cozy place to sit and read once upon a time. Whit imagined Maude McCutcheon sitting in here often, drinking tea, reading her students' essays or story assignments. *Is this where she first read the mysterious manuscript?* he wondered.

"I'm sorry about the mess," McCutcheon said. "We're selling the house, and, as you know, we're trying to get rid of a lot of Mother's things."

"We're sorry to bother you at a time like this," Jack said.

"I was deeply saddened to hear about your mother's death," Whit added. "She was a wonderful woman. A great teacher, in fact."

"Thank you for saying so. She spoke highly of you as well."

"We won't take up too much of your time."

McCutcheon looked perplexed. "You said something on the

phone about a … I'm sorry, I don't remember what you said you found."

Jack opened the brown envelope and took out an old tablet bound on one side with black adhesive tape. The front had a standard black cover with a white panel in the center that said simply, "School Notebook."

"We found this in one of the trunks I bought at the auction," Jack said.

McCutcheon took the notebook and casually flipped through the pages. "I don't recognize the handwriting. I'm sure it doesn't belong to anyone in our immediate family. Do you think it belonged to one of my mother's students? She had a lot of them over the years."

"It's possible," Jack replied. "We were hoping you could tell us."

McCutcheon shrugged. "My sister and I carefully went through everything sold at the auction—and in the trunks. I assume my sister saw this and decided it wasn't worth keeping. What is it?"

"A story."

"It must be an interesting story to have you out on a cold day like this."

"We thought it was *very* interesting, to be honest," Whit agreed. "It piqued our curiosity."

"Why?"

"It's a story about a boy and a girl who somehow slipped from Odyssey into an alternate world."

"An alternate world?" McCutcheon asked. "You mean like another planet or a fantasy world?"

Whit nodded. "Something like that. They wound up in a country called Marus, where they helped a general become a king and seemed to develop unusual powers with the help of a mystical old man."

"Sounds fascinating."

"Fascinating—and possibly *true*," Whit said.

"You're joking."

"Nothing about the story indicated it was fiction." Whit smiled. He knew he must sound like a lunatic.

"If it took place in another world, wouldn't you *assume* it was make-believe?" McCutcheon asked.

Jack chuckled. "One would assume so, yes," he admitted.

Whit lightly brushed his mustache. "Billy," he said, "I run a soda shop for kids in town—"

"Whit's End. I've heard about it."

"One of the things I encourage the kids to do is to use their imaginations. I ask them to allow that sometimes the impossible may be possible."

"You sound like my mother," McCutcheon said affectionately. "But she never came right out and said she believed in other worlds, worlds that are parallel to ours. Do you?"

Whit smiled and shrugged again. "Like I said, I think it's healthy to imagine ways in which the impossible may be possible."

"If nothing else, it's a nice diversion on a cold, wintry day," said Jack.

"How can I help you?" McCutcheon asked.

Whit said, "We were wondering if you found any other notebooks like this one while you were clearing out your mother's things."

"I haven't. But I was going through Mother's financial records mostly. My sister went through Mother's school files and boxes."

"Is your sister here?" Jack asked.

"No. She had to go back to Detroit this morning." He thought for a moment, then waved a hand at Whit and Jack to follow him. They went up the stairs to a small room near the back of the house. It had the appearance of a study, with a desk and bookshelves built into the wall from floor to ceiling. They were empty. "There are some boxes in here that my sister found in the attic," McCutcheon said. "She didn't get a chance to go through them. I think they're more old files from Mother's various classes. You're welcome to have a look if you want."

"Are you sure it's not an imposition?" Jack asked.

"Not at all."

"Thank you."

McCutcheon left them alone to go through the boxes, which were filled with files and papers related to Maude McCutcheon's years as a schoolteacher. Old reports, essays, letters, and awards spanned her career of more than 50 years. Apart from stopping when Whit saw a student's name that he recognized, the two men didn't find anything related to the mysterious manuscript.

"It's possible there was only one story," Jack observed. "We don't know for sure that any more exist."

"I know," Whit said. "But I'd hate to miss the chance of double-checking."

A little over an hour later, they had gone through all the boxes thoroughly. "That's all," Jack said, a trace of disappointment in his voice. He folded his arms and leaned against the desk.

Whit sighed. "Too bad. I had hoped we'd find more." He ran his fingers through his white mane and stretched. "My back is stiff." He tipped his head back to stimulate the muscles in his aching neck.

"I suppose we should go," Jack said, reaching for his coat.

"Wait a minute," Whit said suddenly. His gaze was fixed on the top shelf of the bookcase.

Puzzled, Jack looked up at whatever had caught Whit's attention. "What?" A tiny corner of something—a book? a notebook?—peeked over the edge of the shelf.

Whit reached up and, barely able to pinch it between his fingers, pulled it down. It was identical to the other school notebook Jack had found in the trunk.

Jack's face lit up. "Do you think?"

"I hope so." Whit opened the cover. With a dusty flurry, some papers fell out. Jack picked them up. They were yellowed newspaper clippings.

"Newspaper clippings?" Whit said curiously.

Jack skimmed the articles. "Flu Strikes Odyssey," one of them said. It was from the *Odyssey Times* and dated August 3, 1945. The single-paragraph article reported that a flu epidemic in Odyssey had nearly half the students at Odyssey Elementary out sick. A second article, dated August 7 of that same year, said that many children were still sick with a flu, several were hospitalized, but so far none had died. A third article, dated August 28, 1945, was about the return of Odyssey's "heroes from the war"—men who had fought in World War II and were about to come home. The article also mentioned other families who were still awaiting news about their missing sons, husbands, and friends.

"Interesting," Jack said. "Odyssey had a flu epidemic at the end of World War II."

"I wonder what that has to do with this?" Whit had opened the notebook and was now flipping through the pages.

"Is it another story?"

"It's a story, but I'm not sure that it's—" Whit stopped mid-sentence. "Wait. Yes." He pointed to a word on the page. "Marus. It mentions Marus."

Jack grabbed the notebook they'd brought with them. "Check the handwriting," he suggested.

They held the two notebooks side by side.

Whit smiled. "They're the same. It's the same chronicler."

"Is there a date on that one?" Jack asked.

Whit turned to the first page. "September 18, 1945."

Jack opened the first notebook. "This is dated October 3, 1958. I wonder if they were really written 13 years apart or at the same time and merely dated differently?"

Whit shook his head.

"What do we do now?"

"Talk to Billy," Whit said as he picked up his coat. "And read this story."

Billy McCutcheon was pleased that Whit and Jack had found what they were looking for. After confirming that it wasn't something his mother had written personally, he gave them permission to take the notebook away. Half-jokingly he added, "Just remember where you got it if you make lots of money on the story."

Jack drove Whit back to Whit's End. "I have some errands to run with my wife," Jack said. "You read the story now and I'll pick it up from you later."

"Are you sure?" Whit asked. "You can read it, then bring it back to me if you want."

Jack shook his head no. "Go on," he urged.

Whit said good-bye to his friend and went into Whit's End. It was closed for the day because of all the snow. He had decided it would be good for Connie and Eugene, his two employees, to have the day off. He didn't think many kids would come around anyway since it was such good sledding snow.

In his office, Whit settled down with a cup of hot chocolate and the notebook. He felt an almost childlike twinge of expectation as he opened the cover. Glancing at the three newspaper articles again, he wondered what their connection to the story could be. He put them aside and started to read. "The Chronicle of the Destroyed," it began . . .

CHAPTER ONE

A punch to the stomach sent Wade Mullens doubled over to the ground. Black spots pulsated before his eyes, and he barely heard Steve Calloway mutter, "Kraut-loving freak!" before he walked away.

Bobby Adams rushed up to Wade. "Are you all right?" he asked. His voice seemed miles away.

"I … can't … breathe …" Wade croaked.

"Stay calm," Bobby said. "Relax."

Wade rolled around on the ground, gasping like a fish out of water. After a few minutes, the air came back to him and he sat up.

Bobby knelt next to him. "Oh, boy, you're going to have a shiner," he announced.

Wade gently touched his left eye where Steve had punched him right before the decisive blow to his stomach. He could feel the eye swelling up.

"Can you stand up?" Bobby asked.

Wade nodded. Clasping hands with Bobby, he was tugged to his feet. His legs were wobbly.

"Where are my books?" Wade asked.

"All over the place," Bobby replied. Silently the two boys retrieved Wade's books, which had been littered around the school yard by Steve and his gang.

Bobby, a stout boy of 11 with curly, brown hair, grunted at the exertion of bending over for the books and bits of paper.

Wade dusted the dirt from his blond hair and checked his clothes. A black eye was bad enough, but if he'd torn his trousers or shirt, his mother would have a fit. Apart from smudges of grass and mud, however, they seemed to be all right.

Bobby shook his head. "You shouldn't have said it. How many times did I tell you not to say it?"

Wade shrugged. "I was just stating a fact."

"Fact or not, you can't go around talking about German airplanes as if you *like* them," Bobby said.

"All I said was that the Messerschmitt has a sleek design. What's so bad about that?"

"And you said that the German Me-262 has turbojet power and beats anything we've invented."

"It's true. It has a top speed of 540 miles per hour, and that's a lot faster than—"

"You don't have to tell me! I'm the one who first told you about the Me-262, remember? But Steve's dad was at Omaha Beach on D-Day! You can't talk to people like Steve about the Germans unless it's something you *hate* about them. Otherwise you sound like a traitor."

"I'm not a traitor. Steve's dad came home after the Germans surrendered. My dad is still—" Wade stopped, unable to continue. America had just dropped two atomic bombs on Japan a month before, and the Japanese had surrendered, but Wade and his mother still hadn't heard anything about his father. He'd been missing somewhere in the South Pacific for several weeks.

"You know that and I know that, but Steve doesn't know." Bobby handed him a sheet of paper he'd picked up from the ground. It was a picture Wade had drawn of the B-29 Superfortress, number 77. *The Great Artiste,* it was called. It had carried the second A-bomb to Japan.

In Wade's picture, the plane flew through clear skies. Somewhere below lay the great shipping center called

Nagasaki, represented by a distant shoreline and dots depicting buildings. There were no people in Wade's picture because, like most Americans, he didn't want to think about the thousands who'd died from the two bombs. But, also like most Americans, he was glad that the 20,000 to 40,000 tons of TNT in those bombs had persuaded the Japanese to surrender. Now maybe they'd find his dad and let him come home.

Wade took a moment to assemble his textbooks so he could carry them home. Jammed between the books were comic books about space travel and war, a science fiction novel, and one of the academic journals lent to him by Mr. Curfew, his neighbor. He'd brought that in for show-and-tell, and to tell the class about the various weapons of war. He had told them about the B-17G, the "Flying Fortress Bomber," which was able to carry more than 6,000 tons of bombs over 2,000 miles. He'd also described the Hawker Tempest Mark V, with its ability to go faster than 400 miles per hour; it was one of the few Allied planes that could catch and destroy the German "buzz bombs" (the V-1 jet-powered bombs). Then he'd mentioned the superiority of the Messerschmitt's design and the Me-262's speed. This last part had guaranteed his afternoon fight with Steve Calloway.

Wade had tried to explain to Steve that he didn't like the war or the Germans, but that didn't stop him from learning about the machines and weapons they'd used in the war. Steve wouldn't hear it, and the fists had begun to fly.

"Remember Pearl Harbor!" Steve had proclaimed when he hit Wade in the eye. "Remember the death march on Bataan!" he had then shouted before hitting Wade in the stomach.

Wade and Bobby made their way toward home.

"Do you want to stop by my house to clean up?" Bobby asked.

Wade nodded.

"Good, because there's something I want to show you."

Bobby's mother worked afternoons at Hudson's Drug Store in downtown Odyssey, so the two boys could move around the house easily. Wade gave himself a quick wash in the bathroom while Bobby's younger sister of seven kept asking why Wade's eye was so puffed up. *It looks bad, all right,* Wade thought as he inspected it in the mirror. It was already taking on the tell-tale tones of blue, black, and yellow.

Bobby gestured for Wade to follow him into his bedroom, then nearly closed the door on his younger sister, who whined and protested for a few minutes.

"Look what my cousin sent me," Bobby said quietly. He looked around the room and out the window, then double-checked to make sure his sister was gone before spreading some pages out on his desk. On them were rough drawings of what looked like a large bomb.

"What are these?" Wade asked.

"Top secret," Bobby said.

"Top secret?"

Bobby's voice fell to a whisper. "This is from my cousin Lee in *New Mexico.*"

"So?"

"So! New Mexico is where they've been working on the atomic bomb."

Wade looked from Bobby's face to the pages, then back to Bobby's face again. "You mean ...?"

"My cousin Lee's dad—my Uncle Walter—is a scientist who's been working on the atomic bomb. Lee made these drawings from some papers and photos he'd seen in his dad's briefcase."

Wade's heart lurched. "Are you crazy?" he asked breathlessly.

"There are spies out there who'd *kill* to get their hands on stuff like this."

"Yeah, I know," Bobby said. "Why do you think I'm being so careful?"

Wade pointed to the next page. "What's all this stuff?"

"I think it's how they make them. See?"

Wade glanced over the list: "Uranium 235 ... Uranium 238 ... plutonium ... nuclear fission ... isotopes ... altimeter ... air pressure detonator ... detonating head ... urea nitrate ... lead shield ..."

"Lee said he scribbled down everything he could," Bobby explained.

Wade's mouth was hanging open now. He read about how the various components interacted to cause an explosion. He also saw a page about the effects of radiation on human subjects after the bombs exploded. Many were burned, and some got sick and died. It also warned of radiation getting into water systems and sources of food. "We shouldn't be seeing this," he said finally.

"I know," Bobby said, smiling. "That's why I showed it to you."

"We have to get rid of it."

"I figured I'd throw it in the furnace as soon as we looked it over," Bobby agreed. "Uncle Walt would put Lee on restriction for the rest of his life if he knew Lee had mailed this to me."

Suddenly a voice at the door said, "Bobby?" It was his mother. The door handle turned. Acting quickly, Bobby grabbed and folded the sheets of paper and shoved them under Wade's untucked shirt. "What's going on in here?" Bobby's mother asked.

"Nothing," Bobby answered with a voice that said just the opposite.

His mother eyed him suspiciously, then looked at Wade. "Good heavens! What happened to you?" she said. "Is that a black eye?"

Wade stammered incoherently.

"He fell down on the way home from school," Bobby lied.

"Looks more like you were in a fight," his mother said. "I think you should go home right away."

"But—" Bobby started to protest.

"No 'buts' about it." She put a hand on Wade's shoulder and guided him out of the room. "You go home and get that eye looked at," she instructed him.

Bobby's mother stayed with Wade all the way down the stairs to the front door. He tried to think of a way to get the papers back to Bobby, but Bobby's mother was in the way the entire time. She handed him his jacket and books. Bobby shrugged helplessly at Wade as Wade walked through the door and it closed between them.

On the front porch, Wade zipped up his jacket and pressed his books to his chest. He could feel the papers under his shirt. He looked around nervously. What if there were spies watching him? What if the government found out that Lee had sent the drawings to Bobby and secret agents were coming to arrest them even now? Wade swallowed hard and walked quickly down the steps of the front porch and out onto the street. His walk soon became a run as he took off for home.

Every casual glance from people he passed took on sinister meaning. *They know about the papers,* he kept thinking. A large, black sedan drove past, then suddenly pulled up next to him. *It's them! It's the agents!* Wade thought. The door opened, and Wade cried out—then blushed with embarrassment as an older woman got out of the car to put a letter in the curbside mailbox.

He ducked down some back alleys and zigzagged through his neighborhood, just to make sure he wasn't being followed. When he finally reached his own home, he burst through the front door and raced up the stairs to his room.

"Wade?" his mother called from the kitchen.

Wade dropped the books on his bed, pulled out the papers, and shoved them under his mattress. It was the only place he could think to hide them on the spur of the moment.

His mother called for him from the bottom of the stairs. Forgetting about his black eye, he went back to the top and smiled down at her. "Hi," he said innocently.

"What in the world are you doing?" she asked.

"Putting my books away."

"Why the rush? Didn't you hear me call you from the kitchen?" She wiped her hands on her apron.

"I'm sorry," he said.

"What's that on your face?"

"My face?"

"Come down here," she ordered. Wade went down the stairs to her. She gasped. "Your eye! You've got a black eye!"

"I—"

"Who was it this time, Richard King or Jim McClendon?"

"It doesn't matter," Wade said, shuffling uncomfortably as she ran her fingers gently around his eye.

"Oh, Wade!" she said. "Into the kitchen right now. We're putting an ice pack on it."

Wade groaned.

"And don't make a fuss."

As he walked down the hall toward the kitchen, he suddenly sneezed. It made his eye throb. Then, in the kitchen, he sneezed again.

"Are you coming down with a cold?" his mother asked.

Only then was Wade aware that his nose was running.

❖————————❖

It *was* an illness. And in spite of Wade's protests, his mother insisted that he have a bath after putting an ice pack on his eye and then spend the rest of the evening in bed. As the night progressed, he began to feel worse. By bedtime, he had a full-fledged flu of some sort. His mother made him stay home from school the next day. And the day after. What made Wade feel worst of all, though, was knowing Steve and his gang would think Wade had missed school because of his black eye. When he returned to class, they would call him a sissy and a baby, and the teasing would be far more difficult to take than if they'd gotten into another fight.

In his illness, Wade dreamed of evil-looking men trying to sneak into his bedroom to steal the drawings of the atomic bomb. He dreamed of being arrested by government agents who accused him of being a spy. He saw his name in horrible accusatory headlines on the cover of every newspaper in the country. "Spy!" they said. "Hang him!" the editorials demanded. His mother would live in shame, and his father would never be allowed to come home from wherever he was.

A scraping sound echoed distantly in the register near the door. The sound penetrated his deep sleep. He knew instantly what it was: His mother was in the basement, trying to throw some life into their old coal furnace. From the sounds of it, she wasn't having much success.

Wade swung his legs over the side of the bed and pushed his feet into his slippers. The cool air of the room made him realize his pajamas were slightly damp. His fever had broken, he knew. He stood up, expecting to feel light-headed. To his surprise, he felt normal—good, in fact. His eye didn't hurt as much, either. A glance in the mirror showed him that the swelling was nearly gone and the color wasn't as bad as it had been. He grabbed his robe from the back of the door and suddenly had an idea: Now would be the time to burn the papers about the atomic bomb. He slipped them out from under the mattress, tucked them inside his pajama top, then wrapped his robe snug around him.

"Mom," Wade said when he rounded the furnace in the basement.

Wade's mother looked at him. Her face was smudged with coal. Black streaks also covered her hands, the sleeves of her blouse, and her apron. His mother had never learned the knack of working the furnace, and she got tearfully upset with it. More than once, she'd said that she could endure nearly everything about the war except that furnace. "When your father gets home, we're going to tear it out and get a new one," she'd say. "Do you hear?"

Wade always nodded and agreed.

"What are you doing out of bed?" she asked now, her face flushed.

"I came down to help you."

Mrs. Mullens jabbed a shovel at the inside of the furnace. "I don't need your help," she said. "You should be in bed."

"I'm feeling much better," he replied. He reached up and put his hand on her arm to take the shovel. She frowned, then surrendered the shovel to him. Wade smiled.

"You're the expert, aren't you?" she said as she stroked his blond hair—hair just like hers. "Planes, bombs, and furnaces. Your father is going to be very proud to see how you've grown up."

Wade poked at the fire. "We need more coal."

"He'll be home soon, you know," she said.

Wade turned to her with an expression of understanding. "I know."

But the truth was, he *didn't* know. Neither of them did. The chaos of the war against the Japanese in the Pacific—the many soldiers who had fought on the tiny islands around the Philippines—caused a lot of confusion about who was where. No one was sure what had become of Henry Mullens as the war came to a close. He may simply have been one of many soldiers who'd been separated from his unit. Or he might have been captured, wounded, or killed.

"I would like some tea, please," he said to his mother as he went to the coal cellar in the back corner of the basement. "I'll fix the furnace and then come right up."

She pondered him, then turned to go upstairs. "I hate this furnace," she said as she walked away. "When your father comes home, we're going to—"

"Tear it out and get a new one," Wade called out.

"Brat!" she said with a smile in her voice. He heard her footsteps going up the cellar stairs.

Wade wrenched open the door to the coal cellar. Black soot swirled up and around him. He flipped the switch for the single light that hung by a bare wire from the ceiling. It didn't turn on. "Bulb's out," he said.

Enough light shone in from the furnace room for him to get a bucket of coal, however, so he stepped inside to do just that. Retrieving the empty bucket from where it hung by a peg on the wall, he went to the edge of the pile of coal and started shoveling. Now that his mother was gone, he would throw the papers about the atomic bomb into the furnace with this coal.

He was glad he felt well again. He hated being sick; he missed his talks at lunch, during recess, and after school with Bobby Adams. For the two of them, fascination with the war had taken the place of their fascination with sports. They spoke of the various armed services the way other boys spoke about baseball teams.

He even missed being in his classes, annoying his teachers with his obsession about the war and his extensive knowledge of the weapons and machines that had brought the war to a conclusion. He wondered what they would think if they knew he had top-secret drawings of the atomic bomb.

The doorbell rang upstairs, and Wade heard his mother's footsteps go across the floor. *I wonder who's here?* he thought, and then he suddenly realized, *It may be government agents! They've come to arrest me for having these papers!*

Wade spun around to rush back to the furnace. He could burn them quickly, and no one would ever know. But just then the shed door blew closed.

"Oh, brother," he said in the sudden deep darkness. He made his way carefully to the door and pushed at it. Nothing happened. He pushed again, but it wouldn't budge. He fiddled with the latch, which lifted easily enough, but still the door wouldn't open. He pounded on it and called out, "Mom? Mom!"

He listened, but she didn't reply.

"Mom!" he called out as loudly as he could. Then he pounded some more with the back of the shovel. "Mom!"

He heard heavy footsteps outside the door and relaxed. He was sure that between the two of them, they could get the door unstuck.

The effort wasn't necessary, however. The door suddenly swung open without any problems.

"Thank you," Wade said.

"You're welcome," an old man he'd never seen before replied.

CHAPTER TWO

———✦———

The old man carried a lantern and held it high for a closer look at Wade. His eyes narrowed beneath thick, gray eyebrows. "Heaven help me!" he exclaimed. "What are you doing here?"

"What am *I* doing here? What are *you* doing here?" Wade asked indignantly.

The old man's eyes widened. Wade noticed that they were two different colors, one blue and the other green. "Why, I'm about to feed Bethel," he said.

"Feed Bethel? In my basement?" Wade challenged the stranger. His father had always said that the best way to put off an intruder was by being forceful. Never show fear, he'd said. Wade raised the shovel like a weapon. "Where's my mother?" he demanded to know.

"Your—? I have no idea. Come out of there before you're bitten."

"Bitten?"

"Bethel doesn't take kindly to strangers." The old man gestured to the corner behind Wade. A horse stood there, gazing at Wade with disdain.

Wade stepped back, mouth agape. The coal was gone. Straw and hay covered the floor. Where the bucket had been sitting a moment ago, now sat a trough. The cement wall that had enclosed the coal cellar was also changed; it was now made of wooden slats. "What happened?" Wade stammered.

"Come out now," the old man said patiently. "You've been caught. You may as well confess."

"Confess?"

"You're one of those vandals from town, aren't you? Come to do me mischief."

"No! This is my house!"

"This place may be a lot of different things, but it's certainly not your house." The old man beckoned to Wade. "Come out and explain yourself."

Wade, still staring at what used to be his coal cellar, slowly walked out. His basement was gone, too—no furnace, no workbench, no boxes of keepsakes or the furniture his father had intended to donate to charity. Instead, Wade now looked at what seemed to be a large barn—a *very* large barn, the biggest he'd ever seen. It must have been as long as a football field, maybe even as wide. Along the sides were compartments of stalls, pens, and cages. Pipes stretched the length of the ceiling, some of them feeding down into the various compartments. Lanterns dotted the walls, casting a bright, ethereal yellow over the expanse. Wade blinked, sure that he was dreaming. *I must* be dreaming, he thought. *Why else would I be hearing a lion roar, a pig snort, and a monkey chatter?*

The old man closed the door to Bethel's stall. "Stay put," he said to the horse. "I'll be back."

Wade turned to the old man. He was tall and thin, with a slender, clean-shaved face and a mop of white hair. He wore a long tunic that was belted in the middle. "Something's wrong," Wade said.

"Obviously." The old man reached out and tugged at Wade's sleeve. "What do you call this outfit? The latest city fashion?"

Wade looked down and realized he was still in his robe, pajamas, and slippers. "I'm dreaming," he said.

"Maybe so. Or maybe *I'm* the one who's dreaming. It wouldn't be the first time." He quickly caught hold of Wade's hair.

"Ouch!" Wade cried out. "What are you doing?"

"I wanted to see if it's real." Satisfied, the old man let go.

"It's real. What did you think, I was wearing a wig?"

The old man smiled. "I don't know where you'd ever find a wig that color. Now tell me what you're doing in Bethel's stall."

"I wasn't in Bethel's stall. I mean, I wasn't before. I was getting coal for our furnace, and the door closed behind me and I couldn't get out." Wade spoke as much to himself as to the old man, trying to retrace what had happened.

"I heard you pounding on the door," the old man said, as if confirming that part of Wade's story was true. "But there's no coal or furnace. Just Bethel."

"I must be hallucinating. My fever. That's it. I'm in a feverish delirium." Wade felt his forehead. "But I feel fine. I feel great. This is very strange."

"Listen to the way you talk. 'Delirium.' What kind of boy uses such a word?"

"My teachers say I'm precocious," Wade replied simply.

"Where are you from?"

"Odyssey."

"I've never heard of it."

Wade felt a cold rush go through his body. *Never heard of Odyssey?* He had to think. Either the man was crazy or he was. "Then … where do *you* think I am?" he asked.

The old man chuckled. "It's not where I *think* you are. It's where you are. You're standing in my shelter."

"Shelter."

"Yes, my shelter. How you got in here is a mystery to me, I have to say. We've only got two doors, one that's always locked, except when we're bringing the animals or supplies in. We have to keep a close eye on things, what with the vandals and troublemakers."

"I don't understand."

"Neither do I, but that's the way of things. Let's start with the basics. My name is Arin."

"I'm Wade Mullens."

"Glad to meet you, Wade Mullens, providing you aren't some kind of spy," Arin said, half-bowing to the boy. The word *spy* stopped Wade for a second. He wondered if this strange situation was because of the papers tucked under his pajama top.

"*I'm* not a spy," Wade insisted.

"And this had better not be some sort of trick," Arin warned.

"If it's a trick, it's being played on me."

The old man put a firm hand on Wade's shoulder and directed him onward. "Well, there's no point in standing here asking a lot of confusing questions. We'll get to the truth when you say what you've got to say. Let's go up to the house."

They crossed the floor to a large, steel door that opened to a wide ramp leading upward. At the top, Arin turned a knob on the lantern, and the light faded. Only then did Wade realize that the lantern didn't generate light from a flame, as he had assumed, but from a thin tube. Arin hung the lantern on a hook, then opened another steel door. Wade had to shield his eyes from the bright sunlight outside.

"This way," Arin said, his hand still on Wade's shoulder.

When Wade could see clearly, what struck him first was that he was in a beautiful forest, thick with foliage and rich with growth. He could *feel* the life, if such a thing were possible. And the colors! The greens of the grass and leaves on the trees seemed much greener, the sky above much bluer, the shafts of dancing light through the trees much more golden than he'd ever seen before. It reminded him of the Technicolor films he and his mother sometimes saw at the movies. It was all so much *realer* than real.

He also noticed the sweet perfume of the flowers lining the path ahead. He had no idea what they were, only that they filled the air with fragrances that made him think of vast gardens and fresh-cut lawns. He took several deep breaths as if he couldn't get enough of the scents.

His eye caught Arin watching him. "I'm sorry," Wade said. "It's so … beautiful."

"Yes," Arin said. "This was the first garden. The one from the beginning."

"The beginning?"

"This is where the Unseen One started, when our world was first created."

"I don't know what the Unseen One is."

Arin *tsked* loudly. "And they wonder why our world is so evil! Little surprise that you're a vandal."

"I'm not a vandal!" Wade complained. "Please don't say that. I … I'm either dreaming or I'm lost. I don't know which."

They reached a tall, stone wall and veered around on the path to the right. Directly ahead was a cottage, also made of stone. At the door, Arin paused to touch his forehead and heart lightly with his forefinger before going in. "Muiraq!" he called out.

Inside, the cottage was plain but comfortable in a homey way. The front door opened to a sitting room with a few wingback chairs, a sofa, a coffee table, and a hutch in front of a fireplace. Everything was constructed of dark wood with ornate, carved swirls and curves. Wade instantly suspected it had been handmade.

Up three steps was a dining area and a larger staircase leading to another floor. A woman emerged from a room off the dining area. She wiped her hands on an apron as she entered, giving Wade the impression she was working in the kitchen.

Round-bodied and round-faced, she reminded Wade of Grandma Milly, his father's mother. The thought put him at ease.

"Yes, Arin?" she said. She saw Wade and put a hand to her mouth to stifle a gasp. Composing herself, she simply said, "Oh, hello."

"This is Wade Mullens. My wife, Muiraq."

"It's a pleasure to meet you." She half-curtsied.

"I found him in the shelter. In Bethel's stall, to be precise."

"Honestly? And she didn't bite him?"

"No. I'm surprised, too. But no more surprised than to find him there at all. He has an unusual explanation."

"Does he? Then he should sit down. Is he hungry? I was just preparing lunch."

"Are you hungry?" Arin asked Wade.

Wade wasn't sure, and in the second it took him to think of an answer, Muiraq had already disappeared into the other room. "Of course he is," she said from the kitchen. "What boy isn't?"

"You're going to feed me?" Wade asked as he followed Arin to the dining table.

"The Unseen One would have us treat even our enemies with kindness. And if you're not our enemy, we should be hospitable anyway."

Wade sat down. He wasn't sure he followed the logic of Arin's statement, but he accepted it anyway.

Muiraq returned with a plate of sandwiches, fruit, and cheese. "Help yourself," she said and sat down. Arin poured a sweet fruit juice into wooden cups from a large jug in the middle of the table.

Wade had already put a slice of apple in his mouth when Arin and Muiraq bowed their heads to pray. Embarrassed,

Wade stayed still until the blessing was said, then resumed eating. He was hungrier than he had thought.

"Tell us your story," Arin prompted. "You said you're from a place called Odyssey and that your furnace needed coal." He bit into a sandwich.

Wade started again, telling them how he'd been in bed with a flu and—

"Flu?" Arin asked. "What's a flu?"

"An illness, when you have chills and a fever and runny nose and—" He paused. "You've never heard of the flu?"

"Not the kind you describe. Carry on with your story."

"Anyway, I felt better and went down in the basement to help my mother with the furnace."

"Furnace?"

Wade nodded. "A coal furnace."

"Coal?" Arin's face lit up with surprise. "You use a *coal* furnace?"

"Yes, sir. Don't tell me you've never heard of a coal furnace either?"

"Oh, we've heard of them. We just never met anyone who's used them," Arin said.

"Where is your father?" Muiraq asked.

Wade noticed that her eyes kept going from his face up to his hair and back again. "He hasn't come back from the war yet," he answered.

"War? Odyssey is at war?"

"Not just Odyssey but the whole country. The United States. It was at war with Germany and Japan and their allies."

"I've never heard of any of those countries," said Arin.

"It was a big war. Nearly everybody was fighting in it."

"Was? The war is over?" Arin speared a piece of cheese with his knife and tossed it onto Wade's plate.

"Thank you," Wade said and ate the cheese. It was sweet, unlike any cheese he'd known. He continued with his answer, "We beat Germany, and then we dropped a couple of atomic bombs on Japan, and they surrendered just a few days ago."

Arin and Muiraq exchanged glances.

Wade thought they didn't believe him. "It's true!" he insisted.

"We don't doubt you, lad," Muiraq said soothingly.

"You don't?"

"No," said Arin.

Muiraq turned to her husband. "Do you think—?" she said. "Look at him. Is it possible that he's the sign?"

Arin looked at his wife, choosing his words carefully. "Yes, Muiraq, I believe he is," he replied. "It all fits, doesn't it? The final sign."

"I'm a what? A sign?" Wade asked.

Suddenly, a man with curly hair and beard burst into the room. He said breathlessly, "Come quick, Father. They're—" He caught sight of Wade and stopped midsentence in astonishment. Recovering himself, he continued, "They're back."

Arin was immediately on his feet and raced out the door on his son's heels.

Muiraq sighed deeply. "Why won't they leave us alone?" she asked as she stood up and followed Arin. Unsure of what to do, Wade went along.

The tall, stone wall that served as a fence around Arin's estate had a large, gold gate in it. As Wade approached, he could hear what sounded like a battering ram hitting the gate again and again. Arin and the bearded man were there, along with two younger men and three younger women. They spread out around the gate as if they weren't certain whether it would withstand the blows. Rocks and garbage were hurled at them over the wall, causing them all to duck and dodge. Shouts of abuse were also thrown at them.

"What's wrong? Why are they doing this?" Wade asked Muiraq.

"A drunken mob with nothing better to do with their time, I think," she replied. "It's happening more and more these days."

"What should we do, Father?" the bearded one asked.

"I'll go out and talk to them," Arin responded.

"They'll tear you apart," one of the other young men said.

"They don't have the courage," Arin said. "They're brave as long as this wall stands between us. Face-to-face, they know who they're dealing with. They won't harm me. It's not within their power."

Arin went to the gate. Within its frame was a smaller, man-sized door. He lifted the enormous bar that secured the door and handed it to the bearded man, who struggled against its weight. Only then did Wade have some idea of how strong Arin must be. Arin nodded to his wife, took a deep breath, then opened the door to the crowd. The people went silent at the sight of the old man.

Arin asked in a calm voice, "What do you want?"

No one replied.

"Simply out for an afternoon stroll and some vandalism, is that it?" Arin said with a wry smile.

"We want to know what you're up to behind those walls!" a man shouted.

"You know very well what I'm up to. I've made it clear to you for years now."

"We want to see," challenged a woman.

"Ah, but that you will not do," Arin said and held up his hand. "Repent, turn your hearts to the Unseen One, and you will see. Until then, you'll remain in your blindness and ignorance."

A husky-voiced man called out, "Just who are you to call us blind? Who made you our judge?"

Arin spread his arms as if reasoning with them. "I am not judging you. Only the Unseen One judges. And He has judged you. The wickedness of this generation has reached His nostrils like the stench of a decaying corpse. He has given you every chance to repent, to return to Him. But you refuse. So His judgment is coming. It's closer than you think."

"You've been saying that for years!" another man shouted.

"Yes!" Arin replied. "And to think that you've had all those years to repent, to show good faith in the Unseen One. But have you? No! But the day is coming—it is here!"

A man laughed scornfully. "He's going to wipe us all out, is that what you're saying?" he challenged. "The Unseen One's going to destroy us all!"

Arin turned to Muiraq. "Bring the boy," he instructed.

Muiraq put her hand on Wade's back. Wade resisted when he realized he was the boy Arin wanted.

"It's all right," she said softly. "You won't get hurt."

"Why does he want me?" Wade asked. "I don't have anything to do with this."

"Oh, yes, you do. More than you know."

Wade allowed himself to be guided forward to the door. Anybody who looked like Grandma Milly wouldn't do anything to harm him, he reasoned.

"The final sign is here," Arin announced to the crowd. "See for yourselves." With that, Arin pulled Wade into view.

The crowd gasped and shrank back. Some of them cried out.

Wade wanted to run back inside the gate. He couldn't imagine what was so hideous about his features that people would react that way. He hoped it was the robe. He had never liked the color of it. It had been a gift from his Aunt Priscilla.

"It's a trick!" someone said.

But no one stuck around to find out whether the statement were true. The people backed farther and farther from the door, then turned and scattered in various directions down the street. Many of them kept looking back with expressions of fear. One man lifted a rock and came forward as if he might throw it at them, but Arin's steely look made him think twice. He dropped the rock and ran away.

Arin and Wade stepped back inside. Arin's son secured the door again.

"I don't understand," Wade said. "Why did they act like that? Why were they scared of me?"

"Because of your hair," Arin said.

"My hair?"

"Your golden hair," Muiraq affirmed. "The final sign of the Unseen One's judgment was to be the arrival of a child with golden hair."

CHAPTER THREE

B ack inside the cottage, Arin began to explain, "When I was a young man, the Unseen One spoke to me."

"Wait, please," Wade said. "I still don't understand who the Unseen One is."

"The Unseen One is the creator and sustainer of all things. He fashioned us from the earth, breathed life into us, and chose to love us in spite of our rebellion. He exists in your world, I'm sure. Your world would not exist without Him."

Wade thought about it. "Our 'Unseen One' is called 'God,' if that's what you mean."

"God may be another name for the Unseen One. But in our world, the name *God* is easily confused with the false gods many of the people worship. From the ancient days, we have called Him the Unseen One."

Wade had never thought much about God. His mother and father were good people who seemed to believe in God the way people do when good things or bad things happen. But they never took Wade to church or asked him to read the large family Bible that decorated the end table in the living room.

Arin continued, "The Unseen One spoke to me—"

"How?" Wade interrupted again.

"How?" Arin seemed perplexed by the question. "The same way one person speaks to another. How else?"

"You heard Him?"

"Yes."

"A voice," Wade pressed. "You heard a voice?"

"A voice, yes. *The* voice."

"What did He sound like?"

Arin frowned impatiently. "I wouldn't know how to tell you, lad. I've never found the words to describe it. Nor could I do an imitation."

"I'm sorry," Wade said. "I won't interrupt you anymore."

Arin went on, "He told me that the sins of this generation were more than He could stand. The people have given up His truth for their own lies. He's been repeatedly rejected by His own creation, and He now wishes to begin again. He called me to speak His message of repentance to the people while I built a refuge."

"You mean the shelter I saw, the one underground."

Arin affirmed Wade with a nod. "It is our protection when His judgment comes."

"He *told you* to build the shelter?" Wade still had a difficult time believing that God, or the Unseen One, literally talked to Arin.

"He gave the specific design to me. Every inch, every detail is from Him. I have spent the past 60 years building it. When my sons were old enough, they helped as well."

"There were animals down there, too," Wade said.

"The Unseen One told me to gather the animals, to save them from the destruction."

"What kind of destruction?" Wade's mind continued to try to sort through these facts.

"I don't know. That's something He didn't care to let me in on."

Wade glanced around the room. Everyone in the family stared back at him, their eyes drifting at one time or another to his hair. He felt like a freak. He didn't like being the center of attention. "What about the signs—my 'golden hair'?" he asked.

"Ah, that," Arin replied. "The Unseen One told me that the

wickedness of His creation would increase throughout my life-time. Forces of evil would be invited into the hearts of all mankind, destroying their humanity and replacing it with depravity and decadence."

"That's always the first thing to go when people turn their backs on the Unseen One," Muiraq said sadly. "Their humanity."

"That's because the Unseen One is the source of our humanity," Arin agreed. "Once we have dispensed with Him, we have dispensed with our true selves. So what's left? Men who commit heinous and immoral acts become heroes, giants in the land. Lives become expendable to wicked ideals and causes. We celebrate inhumanity because we no longer under-stand what it is to be human. Corruption spreads to the very root of mankind's being. So the Unseen One said He would lay the ax to the root. He would obliterate what He's created and we—my family and I—would begin anew."

"That makes you pretty lucky, I guess," Wade said.

"Lucky? There is no luck. The Unseen One has chosen us. And as is often true of being chosen, sometimes it is a blessing, but other times it is a curse. I have spent most of my life being mocked and ridiculed. What you saw today was only one small incident. We've had worse. Much worse."

"Arin," Muiraq interjected. "The signs. He asked about the signs."

"Oh, yes," Arin said, recovering himself. "The signs. One was the wickedness of mankind. Another was mankind's rejec-tion of the Unseen One for other faiths and idols. A third was the emergence of corrupt leaders, of which we have many, with not a single faithful person among them. The final was the arrival of a golden-haired child in this land of dark-haired indi-viduals. Until you arrived today, I had always believed it would be a baby. Perhaps one of my sons and his wife would give birth to this golden-haired child. But now you are here."

"But I'm not from the Unseen One. I'm from Odyssey," Wade said. "Don't you see? It's a bizarre coincidence."

"Wherever you are from, however you came here, I have no doubt that you're the one. You're the final sign. It is now only a small matter of time."

Wade's mind was reeling. It was all too much to take in. He looked around the room at their faces. Arin and Muiraq wore expressions of a gentle tolerance, as if they understood more about his doubt and confusion than even he knew.

He glanced at the two young men he'd seen at the gate, now sitting on the sofa. They were Pool and Riv, Arin and Muiraq's second and third sons. Pool was round-faced, like his mother. Riv was slender, with his father's narrow face and sparkling eyes. Next to them were their wives, Nacob and Hesham. Even though Wade was still too young to like girls much, he appreciated that Nacob and Hesham were pretty. One had straight, black hair, dark skin, and penetrating blue eyes; the other had shorter, curly hair, a fairer complexion, and eyes like half moons, as if they were smiling all the time.

Next to the fireplace stood the bearded man who'd come in earlier to tell them about the attack. His name was Oshan. He was the oldest son. He stood quietly while his wife, Etham, sat nearby, knitting an item of clothing. Wade found he couldn't take his eyes off her. She had an angelic face, with wide eyes and a pleasant mouth that turned upward at the corners, as if she were remembering a joke she couldn't tell. Her curly, dark hair fell like waves upon her shoulders. And there was something about her eyes. She reminded Wade of his mother.

Wade stood up and said firmly, "I tell you I'm not from the

Unseen One." His voice caught in his throat. This didn't make sense. None of it did. "Excuse me," he said, then he raced outside to throw up.

When he had wretched as much as he could, Arin appeared with a cup of water for him. He rinsed his mouth, spat, then drank the water in earnest. "Thank you," he said when he could speak.

"You honestly don't know what's happening to you," Arin said sympathetically.

"No. I want to go home. I want my mother." He began to cry.

Arin pulled him close in an embrace that, if Wade had closed his eyes, might have been his father's. "If the Unseen One has brought you here, then perhaps He will take you home, too."

Wade thought that was a lot to ask a kid to believe, especially one who didn't believe in the Unseen One. For all he knew, these people were completely insane. Maybe he'd gone insane, too.

Somewhere in the distance, a low pounding filled the air, like someone banging rhythmically on a bass drum. "What's that?" Wade asked.

"Bombs and anti-aerocraft cannons," Arin replied. "They're trying to destroy the aeroplanes from Belgarum that are bombing the city."

Wade was dumbfounded. "You're being attacked by airplanes?"

"We are at war on all sides," Arin replied. "There are no neighbors to our country anymore, only enemies."

"What kind of planes are they? Spitfires? Mustangs? Messerschmitts?"

"We speak the same language, but sometimes I don't understand a word you say," Arin said with a chuckle.

"I wonder what kind of planes they are," Wade said, trying to be more clear.

"I couldn't tell you. Weapons of destruction never interested me. I couldn't help but feel that they were yet another indicator that the end is coming."

"Are we safe here?"

Arin patted the boy on the back. "The Unseen One keeps His promises. We're safe."

Wade was taken inside and given clothes that Muiraq had made for Riv when he was Wade's age. The outfit consisted of long, cotton trousers, a shirt of the same style as a T-shirt, and a thin robe with a belt covering both. The trousers had deep pockets on the sides, so as he put them on he carefully folded the papers of the atomic bomb plans and slid them into the left pocket. He then strapped on a pair of leather sandals. Wade was impressed with how comfortable the outfit was, and he said so when he thanked Muiraq.

She blushed a deep crimson. "It's my honor to provide them for you," she said. "Now, we'll be eating dinner shortly, so make yourself at home.

"May I look around?" he asked.

"Of course."

Wade's first inclination was to look at the many books on the shelves lining the rooms on the second floor. He was surprised to find that they were printed and bound with a greater quality than any books he'd owned. The reference books—encyclopedias, manuals, and educational texts—had full-color pages and photographs. This was something he'd rarely seen, and only in the most expensive books. The other books covered every topic imaginable: law, medicine, science, the arts, and, mostly, essays and instructions about the Unseen One. Wade skimmed through them all but felt as if they were written in another language. This world—whatever and wherever it was—had a different history from his own. He'd hoped to find an overlap somewhere, something to show that maybe he wasn't in a different world after all. But he couldn't find one, except maybe the being he knew as God and the one they called the Unseen One.

Turning his attention from the books, Wade was curious about the technology of the house. It seemed a lot like his own, until he realized that none of the rooms had power sockets. This wouldn't have been unusual if they didn't have electricity, but they did. Or they seemed to. The lights in the guest room had switches on them. As expected, they made the lights go on and off. But something was wrong.

"Don't you have lights where you come from?" Riv asked when he caught Wade toying with a light in the front room.

"Yes. Just like these," Wade said. "But your lamps aren't plugged into the wall." Wade gestured to the one he had been examining. "See? No wires."

"Should they have wires?"

"How else would the power get to the light bulbs?" asked Wade.

"From the sun."

Wade was confused. "I don't follow you."

"The power comes from the sun," Riv said more slowly. He held up the lamp. On the side was a small, square, silver-colored panel. "This panel receives its power from that panel there." He pointed to a similar panel discreetly placed on the wall, next to the window.

"Where does that panel get its power?"

"From the larger panel above the house. It captures the rays of the sun and transmits those rays as power throughout the house—all over the compound, in fact."

"Then you don't have electricity?" Wade asked, amazed.

Riv laughed. "We haven't needed electricity for years. It's considered primitive now, like outdoor toilets."

"Power from the sun …" Wade mused.

"Unfortunately, because the sun has provided so much, people now worship it instead of the Unseen One," Riv said sadly. "They consider the sun and nature to be the source of life and creation. They no longer believe that the Unseen One provided the natural order to bless us."

Wade pondered it all through dinner. On one hand, this world gave him the impression of being simpler than his own. On the other hand, it seemed to be more technologically advanced. He couldn't think of how that was possible. "May I see the city tomorrow?" he suddenly asked. "I'm dying to have a look around."

"I'm afraid not," Arin said after swallowing a mouthful of potatoes.

"Why not?"

"Frankly, I'm afraid of what they'll do to you."

"Or what you'll do to them," Pool added with a chuckle. "You might cause a riot."

"Then I'm trapped here?"

"You're *safe* here," Arin said. "You're protected here from those who would do you harm or lead you to do harm to others."

Wade fell into a disappointed silence. What was the point of coming to another world and being stuck inside someone's compound?

A messenger from the city elders arrived after dinner. He was heavily bearded and as round as a bowling ball.

"The elders have heard about your guest," the bowling ball said.

"So?" Arin said.

"They want to meet him."

"Then they are welcome to come here."

"You know that's not possible," the bowling ball replied. "Not since ... well ..."

Arin smiled. "Not since I threw them out the last time they came."

"They'd rather the people did not see them come to you," the bowling ball said. "It would make them appear as if they were negotiating with you or giving you respect."

"Which they dare not do," Arin stated sarcastically.

"You understand, I'm sure."

"I understand completely. But they cannot see our guest unless they come here. The choice is theirs to make."

"Must you be so difficult about everything?" the bowling ball asked.

"Indeed I must," Arin replied. "Now, here are some cakes my wife made. They'll comfort your journey back."

The bowling ball's face lit up. "Thank you, Arin," he said sincerely. "And thank Muiraq for us."

"You're welcome, Flabian."

"Who are the elders?" Wade asked after Arin had returned from seeing the bowling ball to the gate. "And from what city?"

"The elders of Sarum," Arin answered as they stood outside the front door of the cottage. "It's our capital city, the city that surrounds us even now. Or maybe I should say that it's the central city of the confederacy."

"What do you mean by 'confederacy'?"

"The simplest way to explain it is to say that the country we're in—Marus, it's called—is a collection of little countries. It's a confederacy of factions or *tribes*. The elders represent those tribes and make the laws accordingly."

"You don't have a president or a king?"

"No. There was a time when the Unseen One was considered our king, but those days are long gone. Now there are elders. However, there is a man who wants to change all that. He wants to be our king, though he hasn't been honest enough to say so directly."

"This is very strange world," Wade said softly.

Arin looked at the boy, then said wistfully, "One day, when the Unseen One's judgment has come and gone and a new generation has risen up, then Marus will be united under a true ruler. But that will be a long time in the future."

"Look at that!" Wade suddenly cried out.

Arin spun around. Wade was staring up at the clear night sky.

"Do you see that?" Wade asked.

"What?" Arin said, looking but not seeing what could have caught Wade's attention.

"There are *two* moons up there! Do you see?" Wade was pointing wildly in excitement. One was large and white, the other nearly half the size and slightly more orange.

Arin laughed, then said, "We've always had two moons. How many moons do you have in your world?"

"Just one."

"How sad," Arin said, then headed back into the cottage.

"May I walk around?" Wade asked.

"Be my guest," Arin said. "But don't leave the compound. Remember what I said."

Wade didn't answer but continued to stare at the two moons. He walked slowly away from the cottage, hoping to see if the sky held any other surprises. He followed the path that took him back toward the shelter. The stars blurred together until he lost interest in them.

The main entrance to the shelter lay just ahead, he remembered. It occurred to him that if he returned to Bethel's stall, it might magically turn into the coal cellar once more and he'd be home again. *But the door will be locked*, he thought. *Arin wouldn't leave it open at night.*

He tried anyway. Sure enough, the door was locked.

Strolling around to the left of the top of the shelter, he noticed how much it looked like the roof of a large and long house sticking up from the ground. It reminded him of a military bunker—made of thick cement and with a gently sloping roof.

He wondered if he could see over the compound wall if he stood at the pinnacle of the shelter. Glancing around, he hoped to find something to climb on, something high enough to get him onto the roof. His eye caught sight of a ladder leaning horizontally against the shelter wall. He ran over to it and was pleased to see that it was at least 15 feet long—long enough to be leaned against the compound wall itself, which was about 15 feet high.

I could climb the ladder to the top of the wall and look out at the city, he thought. Then another idea came to him: *Maybe I could find a way to climb down the other side, check out the neighborhood, then come back again. No one has to know.*

He looked around. Arin and his family were nowhere to be seen. Moving as fast as he could, he dragged the ladder over to the nearest section of wall and hoisted it up. It reached nearly to the top.

Wade's heart raced. Now he'd be able to see more of this new world he'd discovered! He climbed the ladder carefully, but even standing on the uppermost rung, he was still a few feet short of the top of the wall. The only way he'd be able to see over would be to jump up, grab onto the top, and pull himself up the rest of the way.

But then how would he get down again? He eyed the wall, the ladder, and then the wall again. He decided that when he was ready, he could hang from the ledge of the wall and drop back onto the ladder. *Easy*, he thought.

Taking a deep breath, Wade crouched on the top rung, then sprang up as hard as he could. His fingers crooked over the top of the wall. He kicked his legs wildly as he tried to climb up. One of his feet caught the ladder, not just once but two or three times, and knocked it aside. To Wade's horror, the ladder slid along the wall and fell to the ground.

"Oh, no!" he gasped. He waited for a second, then mustered all his strength to pull himself to the top. It was a painfully slow process since his arms weren't that strong. The rough cement of the wall dug into his fingers. He felt beads of sweat form on his forehead and upper lip. He pulled and pulled until, eventually, he worked one elbow over the ledge, then another, and then he swung his right leg up, followed by his left. Finally, he was lying completely atop the wall. He stayed there, panting, for a few minutes.

When he felt slightly recovered, he rolled onto his side. The wall was a couple of feet thick and gave him enough room to sit up. He was facing an alleyway with several tall, brick buildings directly across from him. They looked like warehouses, with large, leaded windows that were now dark and barren of any people or activity. *No view of the city from here*, he thought with disappointment. He looked in both directions and decided to make his way to the right. Maybe he could see more if he followed the wall to that end of the alley. Looking like a squirrel, he scurried along fast as he could on hands and knees. When he reached the end of that wall—and the corner of the compound—he stopped. To his disappointment, he'd come to another alley. *Will I have to scurry all the way around to the front gate in order to see the city?* he wondered.

He decided he wouldn't try. The chances were good that Arin or one of his sons would spot him. Looking back into the compound, he searched for a tree branch he might jump onto. He couldn't see any that were close enough, however, and then he realized Arin was too smart to allow a tree to grow close enough to the wall for an intruder to break in that way.

Wade turned to look in the other direction and only then saw that he was face-to-face with some kind of pole that stuck up from the corner of the wall. At the top of the pole was a rectangular piece of metal tilted down toward the street. It was a sign of some sort. Wade twisted around to get a look at it what it said.

The sign read: "Warning. This is a high-powered security wall." Then it had symbols that looked like lightning bolts, followed by the word *Danger*.

Wade felt his heart jump into his throat. This was a hazardous wall, probably like an electric fence! Yet another way that Arin kept intruders out.

Why isn't it turned on? Wade wondered. *Does Arin have it on some sort of timer? Is it about to come on at any moment and shock the living daylights out of me?*

He tried to decide what to do. He could hang from the side of the wall and let himself fall back into the compound, risking a twisted ankle or, worse, a broken bone. That didn't appeal to him. Maybe he should call to Arin for help, admit he was wrong, and hope they'd let him back in. That didn't appeal to him either. There had to be another way.

Just then, he heard a couple of voices from below. He froze where he was. The voices came from the street, not the compound. Two men walked up the alley, one carrying a flashlight that he occasionally shone along the wall. Wade moved carefully and gently around the sign pole. Suddenly the man with the flashlight flicked the beam up toward Wade. It was a casual gesture; he didn't know Wade was there. But it startled Wade, who jerked back and banged the large sign.

The men stopped and looked up, searching the area with the light. "Who's there?" one of them barked.

"It's someone," the other man said to his partner.

"I guess the power isn't turned on," the first man said.

The second man called out, "Identify yourself! We see you up there."

Wade leaned over the ledge. "It's me," he said. "I mean, it's Wade. Who are you?"

"We're …" the first man hesitated. "Guards, I guess you could say."

"How did you get up there?" the second man asked.

"A ladder."

"A ladder!" the first man growled. "What ladder? We've been around this compound at least twice tonight, and we haven't seen a ladder."

"It's a ladder on the inside, but it fell down."

"So you're saying you're stuck up there?" the first man asked.

"Yes."

The two men laughed.

"It's not funny," Wade said indignantly.

"Don't get snippy with us, boy," the second man said. "What possessed you to get on top of that wall? Don't you know that old Arin could be turning on the power any minute now?"

"I wanted to see the city," Wade explained.

"That's not a very smart way to see it," the first man observed.

"Do you belong in there or out here?" the second man asked.

"In here."

The flashlight beam hit him again, and the two men consulted between themselves in low tones. Wade thought he heard one of them mention his blond hair.

"We could help you," the second man said. "Just crawl down and dangle your legs over. Then let go and we'll catch you."

"Then what?" Wade asked.

"What do you mean?"

"What'll happen to me if I let you help me?"

"We'll take you around to the front gate and let you in."

"How? By telling Arin?"

"No, we'll let you in with our key." The first man held up some keys and jingled them.

"Why do you have a key?" Wade asked.

"You ask a lot of questions, don't you?" the second man complained. "We have a key because we're guards for Arin."

"Really?"

"Yes!" the first man said. "Why would we lie to you?"

"Why *wouldn't* you lie to me?" asked Wade.

"Stay up there and cook, then."

The two men made as if they might walk off.

"Wait!" Wade called out. "I'll trust you."

"All right, just climb over and hang down," the first man instructed.

"Okay." Wade did that very thing: He sat on the edge of the wall, rolled over onto his stomach, slowly slid down until he hung by his fingers, and finally let go. He felt the two men grab his legs, then carry him to the ground.

"That wasn't so bad, was it?" the first man asked once Wade was standing on firm ground between them.

"No, it wasn't," Wade said. "Thank you."

The second man chuckled and said, "You're welcome, you gullible boy."

"Gullible?"

The two men grabbed him with heavy hands. One clamped down on his nose and mouth before he could shout. He couldn't breathe. Then everything went black.

CHAPTER FOUR

Liven, an elder of the confederacy and the only one who actually lived in Sarum, carefully moved the thick black-out curtain an inch to the side. The curtain was designed to keep the meeting room's light from shining outside so the enemy airplanes wouldn't be able to see the building in the dark. In the distance, flares went up and shells exploded like fireworks in the sky. They lit up the skyscrapers and lower rooftops. He wondered what kind of rubble they'd have to sort through in the morning.

"Close the curtain," Acad, another elder, said in a weary drone from the conference table. "It's bad enough that I have to argue with you men. I don't want to die with you."

Liven pulled the curtain tight and turned to the room. *What a sight!* he thought. A blanket of smoke from too many cigars and pipes covered the assembled leaders in a haze. The table, around which they'd gathered, was littered with papers, half-empty coffee cups, filled ashtrays, and food wrappers. *They're pigs*, Liven thought. He frowned. They had been arguing all day, and it looked as if they were going to argue well into the night—all while his beloved city went up in flames. "Can't we stop for a while?" he asked. "My brain hurts."

Dedmon, a heavily bearded man from the Mechlites, wagged a finger at Liven. "I promised my people I would not rest, nor return, without a final agreement," he said.

"I'm not bound by the promises you make," Liven said. He was grumpy now. He would just as readily have assassins kill these men as speak to them. But he needed them; they needed one another to keep from being overrun by their enemies.

"Have we made *any* progress?" Greave of the Kenans asked. He brushed his hand absentmindedly across his bushy, gray eyebrows. They stuck out like wild branches from his thin face.

"We've agreed that we must combine our resources to ward off our attackers," sniffed Krupt. He was from the Shonens, a wealthy faction from the south, and spoke with a thick, stuffed-nose accent.

Acad groaned. "We had agreed on that much before we entered the room this morning!" he complained. "The question is, how much are we each willing to commit?"

"I'm overextended," Dedmon said. "I've poured all we have into battling those pesky barbarians from Gotthard. We're keeping them at bay, but I can't say how long we'll last."

Liven threw his hands up. "Your problem is *everyone's* problem, Dedmon!" he exclaimed. "We're besieged on all sides."

Dedmon picked his teeth casually. "I'm only saying that if we don't come to agreement here, I'll be forced to negotiate my own peace with the Gotthardites."

"You'll have no peace with the Gotthardites," Acad droned. "Only surrender."

"Which will leave the rest of us vulnerable!" Greave snapped.

Dedmon turned on Acad. "It's easy enough for you. You have nothing but sea to the east. What battles do you have?"

"Only the Palatians sending boats from the south, plus the Albanites with their big ships from the north," Acad whined. "They send their marauders in day after day. My coastal towns are panic-stricken."

"If you think the Palatians are vicious on the water, try engaging them on land," Krupt said, then yawned. "Gentlemen,

I will die of boredom if something doesn't happen soon. This gathering was tiresome when it began and has not improved since."

Just then, a knock came at the door. Madalay, Liven's assistant, opened it and peered in. "Sorry to bother you, sir, but he's still waiting," he said.

"Yes, of course he is," Liven replied.

"Who is?" Greave asked. "This is supposed to be a closed meeting."

Liven rubbed his eyes. "It's Tyran."

"Tyran! What's he want now?" Dedmon growled.

"Only to address us for a moment," Liven said. He gestured to Madalay and instructed, "Bring him in."

"I don't trust him," Krupt said simply.

"You don't trust anyone," Greave countered.

Krupt waved a hand to everyone present. "Do you blame me when I have to deal with cutthroats and double-crossers like you?"

The men regarded Krupt and his comment silently. He was right. They were united now only because of their enemies. If they weren't being attacked from without, they would be attacking each other from within. It was the way of the world, Liven thought. In their own way, they were each playing "King of the Hill." A handshake, a stab in the back, and, ultimately, the survival of the fittest: Those were the only rules they lived by these days.

The door opened again, and Tyran strode in.

If nothing else, Liven thought, Tyran knew how to make an entrance. When he walked into a room, he did so with a theatrical flourish and an unmistakable confidence that drew all eyes to him. And yet he was only medium in height and build; his hair was kept unfashionably short; and his skinny mustache—something no one in good society would wear— hung above his thin lips like a black slash on a pasty-white page. His eyes were magnetic, though—black and mesmerizing. His voice was commanding, a deep boom from an otherwise small cannon.

"Gentlemen," Tyran said, gesturing respectfully. "How go the negotiations?"

"None of your business," Dedmon said.

"Not well, then," Tyran said pleasantly.

"You have one minute," Liven informed his guest.

Tyran stood at the head of the table, leaning on the surface with his knuckles. "I will be succinct then," he said. "This confederacy, as you call it, is a joke. You meet for hours and days and accomplish nothing."

The elders reacted with indignation. "Throw him out!" Krupt demanded.

"Throw me out at your own peril," Tyran said, raising a hand to silence them. "I am here to tell you that the *people* are fed up with your politics and bureaucracy."

"People? What people?" Acad demanded to know. "*Whose* people?"

"People from all your districts, the people in the streets," Tyran said. "While you debate and argue uselessly, I have been talking to those you claim to represent. Their confidence and patience are gone. They trust *me* now. I am now the voice you must listen to. I am the one you must respect."

"Nonsense!" said Krupt.

Tyran leaned forward, staring each man down in turn. "I am here to warn you. The people are weary of your ineffectiveness. They are tired of war. They want someone to take charge, to take action. Divided as you are, you cannot accomplish anything."

"And what do you propose?" Liven asked as calmly as he could.

"A united nation. No more factions, no more individual tribes—the Mechlites, the Shonens, the Lahamites, the Kenans. We are the people of Marus, and we should be one!"

"You're living in a dream," Greave said.

"I am living in the *future*," Tyran said. "You may join me or die in the past."

Acad shifted uncomfortably in his chair. "Are you threatening us?" he asked.

"Not a threat but a warning." Tyran spun on his heels and marched out of the room.

"Nonsense," Krupt said again.

Deep crevices formed on Greave's forehead. He stroked his chin. "Is he capable?" he asked. "Does he have the support of the people like he says? My spies haven't reported anything to me about this."

"Your spies are probably working for him," Liven answered.

Greave looked as if he might disagree, but he thought better of it and kept his mouth closed.

Liven addressed the men: "I believe we should take Tyran very seriously. He wouldn't be so emphatic unless he had substantial power behind him."

"It's a bluff," Krupt snorted.

"I'll have some of my men kill him," Dedmon offered.

"And we'll have riots all over the land," warned Liven.

Dedmon was not deterred. "They'll make it look like an accident," he said confidently.

"We'll still have riots," Liven said. "Please, let's put aside our barbaric tendencies for just a moment and consider what we can do to save ourselves. Tyran may well know how the people are feeling, and if we don't take decisive action soon, we may find ourselves on the wrong end of the assassin's knife."

The rest of the elders began to argue Liven's statement. He wearily turned again to the blackout curtain and pushed it aside. To the north, the sky was nothing more than a blood-red stain.

CHAPTER FIVE

Wade was half-dragged, half-carried to a waiting car. There the two men bound and gagged him with a heavy-duty tape. They then threw him into the trunk of the car and slammed the lid down. Enveloped in darkness, Wade woke up and listened as the car pulled away.

A moment later, Wade tried kicking at the trunk as hard as he could. It was solidly shut. He lay still for a minute and tried to think. But there was nothing to think about. He was a stranger in this world, and he had no idea who his kidnappers were or where they were going. So he waited, hoping that someone in Arin's house had heard the noises or the car and was now in pursuit.

From the few seconds he had seen them, Wade knew his captors were dangerous. They had the look of street thugs. What were they doing at the compound? Were they trying to break into the shelter, or had they come for another reason?

The car hummed beneath him. It wasn't the normal hum his parents' Ford made, he realized. This was softer. It lacked the noise of a proper engine. Wade sniffed the air. He didn't detect the telltale smells of gas or exhaust. Was it possible that this car was powered by the sun like so much else in this world?

Nearly 15 minutes later, the car came to a stop. Wade listened as the two men got out and walked to the rear of the car. He considered kicking at them when they lifted the trunk lid, but he realized he wouldn't accomplish much with his ankles and wrists bound the way they were. He'd probably only make them mad, and then they might hurt him.

The lid popped open, and the two men gazed in at Wade. "Hello, boy," the first man said. He had a face filled with deep lines and a drooping mustache. His brown hair was cut close and thinning on top.

"You behave yourself," the second man said with a thin smile on his pudgy face, "and you won't get hurt."

They reached in, pulled him out of the trunk, and leaned him against the car. "I'll hold him while you get him ready," the pudgy one said.

"Right," the mustached man responded. He leaned down and removed the tape over Wade's mouth and, with a quick flick of a knife, from around his ankles, leaving his wrists bound.

"Don't think about running," the pudgy one advised. "You won't get far."

Wade glanced around. They seemed to be in some kind of alley that stretched for blocks between high-rise buildings. A yellow light shone down on them from a nearby door. It reflected off the black sheen of the car. Wade craned his neck to get a better look. The car was like something out of a science fiction comic book. Long and sleek, it had a delicately curved body, with a low top and narrow windows. "Wow," Wade said more loudly than he'd intended.

"You like the car?" the mustached man asked.

The pudgy man laughed and said, "Maybe we'll give you a proper ride in it sometime."

Just then, a bomb exploded in the distance. It sounded closer now than when Wade was in Arin's compound. He was still in Sarum, he knew. But why had they brought him here?

"Let's get him inside," the pudgy man said.

They led Wade into the building through a door marked "Staff Only." The hall was dark, but a safety light ahead allowed Wade to notice the marble floor and the pillars that reached up on both sides to the arches overhead. The style reminded Wade of movies about ancient Rome. He expected Julius Caesar to appear around a corner.

Once more, the scene didn't make sense to him. It was as if this world contained a mixture of styles. Arin's cottage and compound looked as if they had been built in medieval England. His family's clothes, too, were a reflection of that period and style: tunics and robes and sandals. Wade's captors, in contrast, dressed as anyone in Wade's world might have dressed, with worn suitcoats, vests, baggy trousers, and regular-looking black shoes. But against this Roman architecture, they seemed out of place. *What kind of world is this?* Wade wondered as he had before and would again.

"I'm Movan," the mustached man said for no obvious reason.

The pudgy man said, "I'm Simpson."

"You ever need any odd jobs done, you think of us," Movan said.

"That's what we do," added Simpson.

Wade hesitated as a man walked into view ahead of them. He was dressed in a long tunic, just like an ancient Roman senator. *Julius Caesar!* Wade thought.

Movan prodded him on. "No need to be afraid," he said. "It's only Madalay. He's Liven's assistant. Do you know who Liven is?"

Wade shook his head no.

"Only the head of the elders," Movan replied, clearly impressed.

"He's not the head," Simpson corrected him. "Only the host. He's like a … a … mediator for them. Does that make sense to you, boy?"

Wade nodded.

Madalay was directly in front of them now. "You have him," he said.

"We sure do," Simpson said. "Just like we promised."

"He came to us, actually," Movan said.

"Shut up," Simpson snapped as he poked Movan in the ribs with his elbow. "Your messenger created a nice diversion while we sneaked in," he lied to Madalay.

"Good," Madalay said. "Liven is eager to meet him." Madalay took a step back to get a better look at Wade in the light. "His hair. It's astounding. Straight out of a storybook."

"Never seen anything like it," Simpson agreed.

"Liven hopes his appearance will have an impact on the elders. Follow me." Madalay started walking back the way he had come.

"We're going to the elders themselves?" Movan said. "How're my clothes? Not too dirty, I hope."

"Suitably shabby, as usual," Simpson said.

The hallway deposited them into a large reception area. Here the pillars reached way up to ornate balconies far above. At the top was an enormous stained-glass dome covered with pictures of angels and celestial beings dancing in a blue sky. Wade stumbled as he craned his neck to see it all, though it was darkened and the detail was hard to make out.

Simpson tugged at his sleeve. "This way," he ordered.

They walked past large, wooden doors embellished with patterns of oak leaves and vines. Wade's mind went to a field trip he'd taken with his class to the Connellsville courthouse. It had looked something like this, but on a more modest scale. They soon reached a smaller but equally ornate door. A hand-painted sign said, "Chambers."

"Wait here," Madalay ordered, and he slipped into the room. In the moment the door was open, Wade could hear men arguing inside. Madalay's appearance sparked complaints about another interruption. Finally, one man silenced them and instructed Madalay to bring in their guests.

Madalay opened the door wide.

Movan and Simpson stepped forward, blocking Wade from being seen. They smiled proudly to the men in the room.

"Well?" one man droned. "We know these two men. We've all employed their services at one time or another."

Movan and Simpson then moved aside. They obviously wanted Wade to make a dramatic entrance. The group of men—the elders—gasped as if the devil himself had walked into the room.

"He has golden hair!" a man exclaimed as he backed away to the far wall.

Wade felt his face turn red.

"Unbind him," the man in charge instructed Wade's captors.

"Are you sure?" the droning man asked.

Another man wrung his hands and inquired, "Does he have powers?"

"I heard he caused quite a commotion today," one said. "Hundreds of people ran in fear just from the sight of him."

The man in charge said impatiently, "They fled because they are superstitious fools." He spoke to Movan. "Did he offer any resistance? Did he strike you blind or give you boils?"

Movan grinned. "Yes, sir, all of the above," he said sarcastically. "But we recovered."

"Unbind him, then," the man in charge snapped.

Movan quickly undid the tape around Wade's wrists. He was free. But the two men stayed close in case he tried to make a run for it.

"Do you know who we are?" the man in charge asked.

"No, sir."

"We're the elders of Sarum," he said. "I am Liven. That's Greave of the Kenans, Dedmon of the Mechlites, Krupt of the Shonens, and Acad of the Lahamites."

Wade wasn't impressed. "Arin's going to be really mad about this," he replied with as much menace as he could muster.

Liven showed mock concern. "Do you think so?" he said. "Will he call down fire from the Unseen One to rescue you? Maybe the holocaust he has been predicting for the past 60 years will finally come true. Sit down, boy."

Wade sat on a chair next to the wall. All eyes were on him. He didn't like it.

"Where are you from?" Krupt asked.

"Odyssey."

"Where, exactly, is that?" inquired Dedmon.

"The planet earth."

The men laughed.

"As you are a guest, I won't strike you for your impertinence," Liven said. "Next time, I'll forget you're a guest. Now kindly tell us how it is that you're with Arin."

Wade took a deep breath, which caused him to cough. *The smoke in the room*, he thought. When he recovered, he explained to them everything that had happened since he woke up in his bed that morning. *It feels like years ago*, he told himself.

The elders listened to him thoughtfully as he spoke. After he finished, they glanced at one another.

Greave shrugged as if to say, "Well, what do we think?"

"It's more nonsense," Krupt said.

"Everything is nonsense to you," Dedmon complained.

Acad droned, "He's a peasant boy who's been put up to this by Arin. He always said that a golden-haired child would come, and now he's pulled this trick to make us believe him."

"It's probably not the real color of his hair," Greave suggested. "We could arrest him for gross physical alteration."

"I'm telling you the truth," Wade said through clenched teeth.

"To make us believe you're from a different world or time or dimension, you'll have to be a bit more persuasive," Liven stated. "Tell us how your world is different from ours."

"I haven't seen much of your world," Wade responded. "Only Arin's compound."

"Didn't you see our city on the way here?"

"Your goons put me in the trunk of their car."

"I'm sorry," Liven said without meaning it. "Now, what differences have you noticed?"

Wade thought for a moment, then said, "Their car didn't smell."

"Smell like what?"

"Like exhaust, like gas fumes."

"Automobiles in your world do?" inquired Acad.

"Yes."

"My word, are you saying your world uses *petrol-burning* engines?" Krupt asked with an undisguised air of disdain.

"Internal combustion engines, yes, sir."

"Next you'll be telling us you still use electricity!" Greave said with a laugh.

Wade swallowed hard. "Yes, we do."

"You've not harnessed the energy of the provider of our very lives, the source of our very existence—the *sun?*" asked Dedmon.

It was Wade's turn to ask, "Do you use the sun for everything?"

"Of course we do!" Dedmon replied. "It drives our autos, our aeroplanes, our ships. It provides energy to our homes and buildings, gives us light by night, coolness for hot days, warmth for cold ones. It is … everything."

"Even your weapons?"

Liven said quickly, "We're still developing our weapons. War was fairly unknown to us until the last hundred years. We were too busy developing our arts, sciences, and medicines."

"What kind of weapons do you have in *your* world?" Krupt asked Wade.

Wade thought about it for a moment. "Rifles, machine guns, hand grenades, torpedoes, artillery cannons, bombs—"

Liven gestured wearily. "That's more than enough," he said.

"What kind of bombs?" Acad asked.

"The kind that explode."

Acad was not amused but said sarcastically, "What sorts of bombs do you use: *gas*-powered bombs? Electric bombs, perhaps?"

Wade was tired of being made fun of, so he said to impress them, "We have atomic bombs."

The elders looked puzzled. "What kind of bombs?" Liven asked.

"Atomic," Wade repeated.

"You're going to have to explain that to us," Liven said.

Wade feigned boredom, like a teacher with silly school-children. "It's based on nuclear fission," he explained. "You see, the bomb is made of plutonium or uranium, and neutrons are shot into it, which causes a chain reaction, and then *boom*, the explosion. It could destroy your entire city in just a few seconds."

The men sat silently, assessing what Wade had said.

"Your world has obviously spent a lot of time developing its warfare," Liven observed.

"Or your imagination has!" Krupt snorted. "I don't believe

a word of this drivel. This boy is making it all up. Uranium, plutonium, chain reactions … it's nonsense!"

Krupt's statement triggered a chain reaction of its own as the elders began to argue among themselves. They were divided over whether or not to believe Wade. This then spun into a debate about what to do with Wade now that they had him in custody.

"You have to take me back to Arin!" Wade insisted.

Liven shook his head. "Arin will wait," he said. "If you are who you say you are, a boy from another world, we dare not let you loose. If you aren't, we dare not allow Arin to wreak havoc among the people by using you as a means to frighten them. Morale is low enough right now. We can't have Arin's message of doom and gloom taking it any lower."

"But what if he's right?" Wade asked.

"Right!" Greave cried out. "He's a lunatic! He can't be right!"

Liven signaled to Movan and Simpson to take Wade out. "Take him to the security house," he ordered. "Keep him there until I tell you otherwise."

"Yes, sir," Simpson said.

"You're making a big mistake!" Wade shouted to the elders as he was taken away. Madalay closed the door behind him, cutting off their laughter.

Madalay said, "You have your instructions," and walked away.

"We have our instructions all right," Movan said with a smile filled with gray teeth.

When Madalay was out of earshot, Simpson added under his breath, "Too bad they aren't the instructions Liven gave us."

CHAPTER SIX

W̲ade was taken back to the car, but this time he was allowed to sit between Movan, who drove, and Simpson. The seat was plush and comfortable. The car's dashboard was lit up like a Christmas tree, with red and green lights next to symbols Wade didn't understand. Movan pushed a button, and the car drifted forward, as if on air.

"Is it fast?" Wade asked.

"Is it fast!" Movan said with a chuckle. "You just watch." He moved the steering column forward slightly, and the car took off. They flew down the city streets, past large skyscrapers and smaller office complexes, all with the same Romanesque architecture. But street lamps burned yellow nearby. *It's like Rome with electricity*, Wade thought.

They zoomed past other cars with body styles similar to the car they were in. Wade looked carefully to see if the cars were actually riding on tires. The ride was so smooth that he doubted it, but the tires were there, spinning quickly underneath.

Simpson frowned. "Stop showing off," he said. "If you get us pulled over, we'll be in big trouble."

"How can we get in trouble if we're on official business?" Movan asked.

"If we were going to the security house, we *wouldn't* get in trouble," Simpson said slowly. "But we're not going there. Remember?" Simpson reached over and tapped Movan's temple. "We're going to Tyran's castle. Remember?"

"Oh, yeah," Movan said, slowing the car down.

"Tyran's castle?" Wade asked, perplexed.

Simpson glanced down at Wade. "We got a better offer for you," he said simply.

They drove south, reaching a spacious section of the city where the skyscrapers and offices gave way to homes scattered on large plots of land. At the top of a large hill sat a genuine castle with a moat, a gate, turrets, and towers peering at them majestically from all sides.

"It *is* a castle!" Wade gasped.

"Would we lie?" Movan said.

"Who is Tyran, and why does he want me?" asked Wade.

Simpson replied, "He's one of the richest and most powerful men in the city. As for why he wants you, that's for him to know and you to find out."

A winding lane took them up to the castle gate. Triggered by some unseen signal, a drawbridge lowered smoothly over the moat. They drove inside and parked in a large courtyard. A man with short, dark hair and a thin mustache strode up to the car as they climbed out.

"Tyran," Simpson said and bowed slightly.

"I am glad you made it safely," the man said formally, then looked at Wade. "You are our alien visitor, I take it."

"My name is Wade Mullens."

"I know," Tyran said.

"So, what now?" Simpson asked.

"You are to make it look as if someone attacked you and kidnapped the boy," Tyran said. "It would be best if everyone thought Arin or his sons had done it."

"Oh, no, sir!" Movan pleaded. "Our reputations will be ruined if people think Arin and his sissy sons stole the boy from us."

Tyran gazed at him with a steely expression. "Your vanity is no concern of mine," he said. "Do as I say."

Simpson sighed sadly. "You heard him, Movan," he said miserably. "We have to make it look like we were attacked."

"As you wish," Movan said, then punched Simpson in the jaw.

Simpson staggered back, then returned with a hard right to Movan's eye.

With grunts and groans, the two men pummeled each other. Tyran led Wade into the castle as they continued.

"The elders are a collection of idiots," Tyran said. "I heard how they treated you in that meeting. Abominable! They have a guest from another world in their midst, and do they treat you with respect? Do they listen to you? No. They disbelieve and ridicule you. A travesty!"

"How did you know that?" Wade asked.

"How do I know what?"

"How they treated me. You weren't there."

A shadow of a smile crossed Tyran's face. "I have listening devices in the room. I would not let those buffoons gather together without knowing what they were saying."

Wade shuddered as a cold chill shot through his body. *Why did he tell me that?* he thought. *How does he know I won't tell the elders about his listening devices? Unless he's planning to keep me here …*

"Are you hungry? Would you like something to eat?" Tyran asked.

They locked eyes for a moment, and Wade felt instantly drawn in by them. They were friendly eyes, the eyes of a compassionate preacher or a good-natured uncle. He saw nothing to be afraid of in those eyes. "No, thank you," Wade replied.

"Then allow me to tell you what is going on here," Tyran said as they strolled down a long hallway lined with suits of armor and brilliantly colored tapestries. "I am a man who has grown very tired of the various factions, tribes, fiefdoms—call them whatever you want—that have divided Marus for too many years. I think it is time that they are united under one vision, one leader."

"You want to be that leader, right?" Wade said, thinking of another leader who had said the same kind of thing and led his world into war.

Tyran nodded. "From my childhood, I knew this was what I was called to do. I was chosen to bring our nation together."

"Chosen by whom?"

"Fate. Destiny. The Almighty Sun. You choose a name."

"The Unseen One?"

"You may use that name if you like. I do not believe in Him myself. But it is a suitable name for whatever power makes things happen in this life." Tyran gestured to a large doorway. They walked in. The enormous room had lavish antique furniture, wall-sized bookshelves, and a harpsichord.

"Why did you bring me here?" Wade asked.

"Because, like Arin, I believe your coming is preordained. I believe you are from another world and have been sent to our world to bring about a new age."

"Arin thinks I'm the final sign of the end of the world."

"That is Arin's opinion," Tyran replied dismissively as they continued walking toward the far side of the room. "But I think you are the final sign of the *beginning* of the world. That sounds so much better than Arin's idea, does it not? Would you not rather help *start* something than end it?"

"Well … yes," Wade said.

"I thought so." He smiled at Wade. "I suspect that you and I are not so different. In you, I see myself as a boy. I will wager that you get picked on at school. The other children do not understand your intelligence. The teachers do not know what to make of you."

Wade was silent. It was all true. Bobby Adams had said that Wade was too smart for his own good. His mother said the same thing.

Tyran placed a gentle hand on Wade's shoulder. "Those days are over. Everyone who works with me will appreciate you. They will understand the gift you are to us. You were brought here to help me unite the world in peace."

"How?" Wade asked, wanting to believe him but remaining skeptical. "I'm just a kid."

"You are not just a kid," Tyran challenged. "You are a visionary, like me. I heard what you said about your world and its weapons, your description of that bomb—the one that can destroy an entire city within seconds."

"The atomic bomb?"

"Yes. If you can tell us about that, there are other things you can tell us. The weapons from your world may help our world. They may help me to bring about peace."

"I only know a little about them," Wade said. "I don't know how to *build* them."

"Do not worry about that. I have a very smart man who will take care of the construction. All you have to do is tell him everything you know. Somehow we will find a bridge between our inferior weapons and your superior technology."

"What man?"

"Dr. Lyst."

They had arrived at a door on the far side of the large room, and Tyran now threw it open, revealing a huge laboratory filled with electronic gadgets, beakers on burners, test equipment, and blackboards with complex formulas written from one edge to the other. At the far end of a lab table, a man in a white coat stood bent over a microscope.

The man straightened up and quickly approached with a broad smile and outstretched hand. "Is this him?" he asked.

"This is Wade," Tyran replied.

The man shook Wade's hand vigorously. "A pleasure to meet you," he said. "I've never shaken hands with someone from another world!"

"It feels the same as anywhere else," Wade offered.

The man laughed. His slender face reminded Wade of an exclamation point. Something about his expression was bright and alive.

"I am Dr. Lyst," the man said. "You and I will be working together, I understand."

"Only if Wade wants to. He has not said he will," Tyran explained, then gazed at Wade. "If you want to go back to Arin, now is the time to say so. I will not stop you. But I think your purpose in this world will be better fulfilled here with us."

Wade didn't know what to say or do, and he had already forgotten Tyran's last instructions to the kidnapers. "I'm a stranger here," he replied after a moment's hesitation. "I don't know where I belong."

"Then you may as well stay with us," Dr. Lyst said.

"I guess so."

Dr. Lyst suddenly flapped his hands at Tyran in a shooing motion. "Go away now," he said playfully. "He's mine."

Tyran laughed and said, "I look forward to seeing what you two come up with."

"Yes, yes, now go away." Dr. Lyst walked Tyran to the door and saw him out. He closed it firmly, then turned to Wade. "This is going to be fun," he said with a smile.

CHAPTER SEVEN

Dr. Lyst's face was ageless. Wade guessed he was in his forties but couldn't be sure. He had black hair, with gray at the temples that made it look as if his head had grown wings. He also had a smooth, babylike complexion; the only lines were the crow's-feet that had gathered at the corners of his green eyes. He was square-jawed and had high cheekbones, which gave his wide mouth room to smile in a big way. Wade found the face reassuring.

"Let's sit down and you can tell me everything," Dr. Lyst said, pulling a chair close. He had an expression of pure delight on his face, as if he'd just made a brand-new friend. "I read the transcript of your statement to the elders."

"Transcript?"

Dr. Lyst motioned with his thumb toward some papers on the table. "Word for word. Everything you told them. I'm fascinated. I could spend days—*weeks*—trying to figure out how you got here. Just think what it would be like if we could jump at will from place to place, dimension to dimension."

"You believe me?"

"Why wouldn't I? You're here, aren't you?"

"But I could be from this world. I could be lying to all of you."

"Not with that hair you aren't."

"You don't have blonds—er, people with golden hair—in this world?"

"Perhaps in some undiscovered part somewhere. And if you were from an undiscovered part, it would be the same as if you had come from another world. Why does it bother you that I believe what you said?"

Wade shrugged. "I keep thinking that I must be dreaming. I'm going to wake up in the coal cellar with a bad fever."

"Ah! Thank you for reminding me," Dr. Lyst said. "I want to do a quick physical on you, if you don't mind."

"A physical? Why?"

"To see if you're made of the same stuff as we are: flesh and blood."

"I am."

"I'll be the judge of that," Dr. Lyst said playfully. He reached into a nearby drawer and pulled out a small box. He opened it and retrieved what looked to Wade like a stethoscope and a blood pressure gauge. "This won't hurt a bit."

"What are you going to do?"

"Check all your vitals." Dr. Lyst touched a button on the side of the box, and the inside of the lid lit up in a colorful array of blues, reds, and greens. Then they faded to gray. Wade looked closer at the lid and realized it was a small transmission screen. He had seen the new television sets at a downtown appliance shop, but he didn't expect to see anything like that here. "Is something wrong?" Dr. Lyst asked.

"Is that a television?" Wade asked in a whisper of wonder.

"It's a monitor." Dr. Lyst picked up the stethoscope. But rather than put one end of it in his ears like the doctors in Wade's world, he plugged it into the side of the box. The screen came alive again with colorful charts and graphs. "Stand up, please."

Wade obeyed. Dr. Lyst held the coinlike end of the stethoscope between his fingers and began to move it a few inches from Wade's body in a scanning motion. He went from head to foot and side to side. Dr. Lyst watched the screen in the box.

"You had your tonsils removed," the doctor said.

"When I was five."

"You did something to your knee?"

"I cut it once and had stitches."

"Seven, to be precise. And you've been sick recently?"

"I had the flu."

"Flu? Hm. I don't know what that is, and neither does my scanner."

"I feel better now." Wade was amazed. "This gadget is telling you all that?"

"That's what it was built to do," Dr. Lyst said. "Don't you have them in your world?"

"No, sir."

"Too bad." Dr. Lyst put down the stethoscope. "You seem to be in normal physical health as far as your skin, tissue, and bones are concerned. I'll make a note of the 'flu' you mentioned." He picked up the blood pressure gauge. "Hold out your arm, please."

Wade stretched out his arm.

Dr. Lyst rolled up Wade's sleeve, then wrapped the pressure cuff around his arm just above the elbow. Again, he plugged the other end into the side of the box. Wade felt as if someone had a tight grip on his arm.

"Is this reading my blood pressure?"

"It's reading your blood pressure and taking a blood sample."

"You mean, right now?"

"Yes."

"But shouldn't I feel a prick or something?"

"No. It was designed to take the blood without you realizing it." The box beeped at Dr. Lyst. He took the pressure cuff off Wade's arm. "All finished. The analyzer needs a little while to evaluate your blood, but all in all, I'd say you're no different from a normal, growing boy in our world."

"This is amazing."

Dr. Lyst put the box away. "Now let's talk about your world," he suggested. "Tell me everything."

Wade didn't know where to begin and shrugged helplessly.

Dr. Lyst smiled warmly. "Why don't you start with your family? Tell me about your mother and father, your brothers and sisters."

"I don't have any brothers or sisters," Wade explained. "It's just my mother and me until my dad comes home from the war."

"What does your dad do in the war?"

"He's a pilot, stationed in the South Pacific. But we don't know where he is right now."

"Why's that?"

"We haven't heard from him—nobody has—for a few weeks. All the other dads have contacted their families in Odyssey, but my dad hasn't. We don't know why. Mom keeps calling and asking, but nobody knows where he is right now."

"You're worried."

Wade nodded.

"How did your country ..." Dr. Lyst's brow creased with sudden concentration. "What's it called?"

"The United States of America."

"Tell me how it became united, and then tell me why it went to war with the South Pacific."

Wade laughed. "It didn't go to war *with* the South Pacific. It went to war with Japan and battled the Japanese *in* the South Pacific. The South Pacific is an ocean. Here, I'll show you. Do you have some paper and a pencil? I'll draw it."

Wade drew a rough map of the world for Dr. Lyst and identified which countries were on whose side in the war. He explained about the Germans and the Japanese and the Italians, the Americans, the British, the French, and the Russians. He drew the United States and England to explain how the colonies became independent back in 1776 and had been dedicated to fighting for freedom ever since.

"So, the United States and its allies defeated Germany and Italy by sheer force and skill in battle, then resorted to dropping the atomic bombs to make Japan surrender?"

"Yes, sir."

Dr. Lyst drummed his fingers on the tabletop. "This is Tyran's goal, you know."

"What is?"

"To create weapons that are so superior to our enemies' that they'll have to unite with us or negotiate a peace. It's identical to what your leaders did." Dr. Lyst's eyes lit up. "Your arrival here is a … a miracle of sorts."

"I'm glad everyone thinks so," Wade said, feeling proud of his importance.

Dr. Lyst gazed earnestly at Wade. "You help us, Wade, and I'll do everything I can to get you home. I promise. Now, tell me about your technology."

Far into the night, Wade told Dr. Lyst everything he could. And when he finally felt certain he could trust Dr. Lyst, he pulled the drawings of the atomic bomb from his pocket. "Here," he said simply.

"What are these?"

"Drawings of the atomic bomb and"—he pointed to the other page with the list—"some of the materials they used."

Dr. Lyst peered at them for a moment. "Where did this information come from?" he asked. "How are you so privileged?"

"The father of a cousin of my best friend worked on the bomb. The cousin made these drawings from papers in his dad's briefcase for us to see."

"Why would he do that?"

Wade shrugged. "Because he knew we'd be interested."

"Fascinating! Crude, but fascinating."

Wade yawned and rubbed his eyes. Dr. Lyst noticed and said, "That's enough for tonight. You're tired. May I hold onto these?"

"Yes, sir. I was going to burn them anyway."

"Why?"

"Because the atomic bomb is a big secret in my world. I was afraid I'd get arrested or kidnapped by spies." Wade chuckled. It all seemed so silly now.

Dr. Lyst reached over to a button on the wall and pushed it. A servant seemed to appear from nowhere. "It's time to show this young man to his room," said the doctor.

The servant, a stiff-gaited old man, nodded. "Come along," he told Wade. He took Wade down another long hallway to a bedroom. It was luxurious, with a four-poster bed and velvet curtains, dark paneling on all four walls, paintings of rolling hills and countryside, an enormous fireplace with a marble mantelpiece, and two chairs and a table by a tall window. The servant pointed to a door next to the fireplace and said, "The bathroom is in there." He then pointed to a cord hanging next to the bed. "If you want anything, anything at all, simply pull that cord and someone will be here immediately to serve you."

"Thank you," Wade said.

A tabby cat suddenly leapt up onto the bed and meowed at Wade.

"That is Cromley," the servant said. "If he's a nuisance, I can put him out."

"He's all right," Wade said and scratched Cromley on top of his head. Cromley pressed himself against Wade and purred.

The servant retreated from the room, closing the door

behind him. Wade wanted to have a look around, but he made the mistake of trying out the bed first. He lay down and absent-mindedly stroked the cat. His last thought as he fell asleep was that life in this world might not be so bad after all.

Dr. Lyst stood in his laboratory and watched Wade on a screen, which had been hidden behind a curtain on the wall. Tyran walked into the room and stood next to the doctor.

"Well?" Tyran asked.

"I believe he's the genuine article," Dr. Lyst answered as he stroked his chin thoughtfully. "No one could come up with such an elaborately constructed fantasy world as he has. Certainly no one at his age. It all makes sense. He comes from some other place and time. I don't know how, but he has."

Tyran smiled. "Will you be able to take what he knows and turn it into something we can use?"

"I'll do my best," the doctor said.

Tyran patted him on the back. "Of course you will. But you know that time is working against us. If we're invaded …" he began, leaving the thought hanging.

"I'll work as fast as I can."

CHAPTER EIGHT

❧————————————————❧

W ade was awakened by the sound of running water. He slowly sat up in bed. The servant who had brought him to the room the night before was in the bathroom. It sounded as if he was filling the bathtub. The servant emerged and looked pleased to see Wade awake.

"Good morning, sir," the man said.

"Good morning, sir," Wade repeated, stretching his arms.

"Your bath will be ready for you in a moment."

"Thank you. But you didn't have to go to any trouble. I could've run the bath myself."

"It's what I do, sir."

"Oh. What's your name, if I'm allowed to ask?"

"I'm called Thurston, sir."

"It's nice to meet you, Thurston." Wade scooted out of bed and shook Thurston's hand. "I'm Wade."

"Yes, sir. Did you sleep well?"

"Like a log."

"I assume that's a good thing?"

"Yes. Very good."

"I'm glad to hear it. Dr. Lyst is waiting for you in his laboratory after you've had your bath and breakfast. He seems quite eager to begin working with you today." Thurston began to make the bed. "I must say, I've never seen him like this."

"Like what?"

"Well, he's like a little child with a new toy."

"Am I his new toy?" Wade asked.

"I suppose you are, in a manner of speaking, sir." Thurston

hesitated, clutching the bedspread. "If you don't mind my saying so, the entire castle is talking about you."

Wade self-consciously touched his hair. "Because of my hair, right?"

"I suppose for some. But most of them are talking about your knowledge. I'll speak honestly, sir: You have brought a tremendous amount of hope with you to this place."

"Me?"

"Yes, you. I dare say that you've become something of a celebrity."

Wade was impressed. "A celebrity," he repeated softly.

After his bath, Wade was given new clothes to wear. Unlike the tunic he'd worn at Arin's, he was given laced shoes; normal-looking, gray trousers; a plain, white shirt; and a V-neck sweater. Standing in front of the mirror, he thought of pictures he'd seen of students who go to colleges like Oxford or Cambridge in England. Thurston then took Wade to a large dining room where he was served eggs, toast, bacon, orange juice, and cereal. It seemed like ages since he'd eaten so much in the morning.

Dr. Lyst was pacing anxiously in his laboratory when Wade arrived. The doctor stopped in his tracks and smiled broadly. "Hello, young man," he said. "Did you sleep well?"

"Very well, thank you."

The doctor picked up a clipboard and assembled some sheets of paper on it. "We have a lot of work to do today," he said eagerly.

"We do?"

"I have to get everything I can out of that brain of yours."

"What if I don't know as much as you think I do?"

"But you do," Dr. Lyst said matter-of-factly. "It's all in there. I'm confident of it."

Wade grinned. If only the kids at school could see him

now! They wouldn't dare laugh at him for the science-fiction comic books he was nuts about or the stolen moments at lunch and recess with the science journals that Mr. Curfew, his next-door neighbor, lent to him. The kids thought he was weird and often said so to his face, but now he was *important*. Oh, if only Steve Calloway could see him!

"Let's talk specifically about how explosives were developed in your world," Dr. Lyst said.

"All right," Wade replied. "But I'm a little rusty with my history."

"Do your best. Think hard. If I can establish any parallels between your technology and ours, I may be able to find the means to create here what you have created there. Now, tell me everything you can."

Wade took a deep breath. "Let's see … I think it all started with gunpowder."

"What's it made from?"

"Oh. Let me think. It's been such a long time since I read about that. Saltpeter and charcoal and sulfur."

"What is saltpeter?"

Wade had to think for a minute. Then it came to him: "Potassium nitrate. When you put all three together, it creates a black powder that—"

"Ah! Black powder."

"That's one of the names for it."

"It certainly was," Dr. Lyst said. "It's mentioned in the writings of our forefathers. But the exact formula has been lost for ages."

"Then what are you using now?" Wade asked.

"Solar bombs."

"You mean, you're using energy from the *sun* for your bombs?"

"Precisely. We created a catalyst that makes the solar cells explode. Not unlike the black powder, I suspect."

Wade was mystified. "That's what the planes are dropping at night?"

"Yes," Dr. Lyst said. "But we've gotten as much out of them as we ever hope to. They're a peacetime technology that's ill-suited for war. They don't have the power we need. Some explosions, fire, and a little bit of damage. That's all. It's more for show than for destruction."

Wade shook his head. "I just don't get it. This world seems so … so advanced with some things, but so backward with others."

Dr. Lyst folded his arms, his clipboard pressed against his chest. "You have to understand that war hasn't been a priority for us. For the most part, our nations have gotten along over the years. We had skirmishes and fights every now and then, but not major wars. Not until now. Now everyone has a blood-lust for power. Treaties are broken; trust is destroyed. Neighbor has turned against neighbor."

"Arin says it's because everyone lost their faith in the Unseen One."

The doctor grimaced. "That's just the sort of thing I would expect Arin to say," he responded with obvious distaste. "This has nothing to do with the Unseen One. It has to do with us —with the abuse of power. Tyran wants to change all that."

"By being the most powerful, right?"

"Power in the hands of a benevolent man like Tyran is a good thing."

Wade said carefully, "There's a saying in my world: Absolute power corrupts absolutely. Or something like that."

"That may be true in your world, but not with Tyran. I've known him most of my life. His vision for unity and peace is real. But he's no fool. The only way to impress these barbarians who call themselves our leaders is to carry a bigger stick than theirs. Now tell me: Your world started its explosives with black powder, but what was used after that?"

"Have you ever heard of dynamite and nitroglycerin?"

Their discussion went on from there. Wade told him all he knew about the discovery of nitroglycerin in 1846 by an Italian named Ascanio Sobrero. Dr. Lyst laughed when Wade mentioned that it had originally been used as a headache remedy. But it was too dangerous for Sobrero to use for blasting, so he gave up. In 1862, Alfred Nobel of Sweden began to experiment with it, accidentally killing his own brother in the process. But he persevered, and, in 1866, he successfully mixed liquid nitroglycerin with an absorbent substance called diatomite. As a result, dynamite was born. After that came TNT.

"TNT?" Dr. Lyst asked as he scribbled on his clipboard.

Wade rubbed his forehead. His head ached. "That stands for … for … tri-nitro-toluene. Or tri-nitro-toluol. One of those two. It comes from coal tar or gasoline, I think."

"Don't stop, keep talking," Dr. Lyst encouraged him, writing furiously.

"All the explosives and bombs we use are directly related to TNT," Wade continued. "There's dynamite and amatol, which is TNT and ammonium nitrate. There's ammonal, which has powdered aluminum, TNT, charcoal, and … and ammonium nitrate."

"Go on."

"I read that scientists just developed some new explosives in the war. Something called RDX, which is … is … hexamine and TNT. And something else called pentolite. That's some other mixture with TNT. I don't remember."

"Try."

"I can't. My head hurts."

"What do these explosives have to do with the atomic bomb?"

"Nothing."

"Nothing!"

"The atomic bomb is completely new. It's a whole different idea. But I wouldn't know how to explain it," Wade said.

"You explained it to the elders."

"Those were just the pieces. It's top secret. Most of us didn't even realize the bombs existed until we dropped them on Japan. We'd heard about tests in the desert and hush-hush goings-on in the government, but we never thought …" His voice faded. He rubbed his eyes wearily. "You have the drawings. That's as much as I know."

"That's enough for now," Dr. Lyst announced as he tossed his clipboard onto a lab table. He patted Wade on the back. "Well done. I'm sorry to push you so hard, but time is very important to us."

"But I didn't tell you anything."

"You told me a lot more than you think. I can now point my technicians in the right direction, which is something I couldn't do before. We don't have to start entirely from scratch. We have an idea of what we're looking for."

Wade stood up. His legs were stiff from sitting on the stool. "Do you really think you can create an atomic bomb?" he asked.

"I don't know. But you've given me the stepping-stones that your world walked on to reach that end. *Anything* we develop now is bound to be more powerful than the solar bombs."

"I hope so. My brain can't take very much of this."

"I'm sure it can. But you've done an amazing job this

morning. I'm very proud of you." Dr. Lyst was standing at the window now. "Would you care for a walk to clear our minds for a while? It's a beautiful day."

❖————————❖

The golden sun lingered high above them, a large dot in the middle of a clear sky. From the walk along the castle wall, Wade could see the entire city of Sarum. Skyscrapers, government buildings, hotels, and shops rose impressively from the ground in an array of formations and styles. The scene reminded Wade of the view he'd had of New York City from the Empire State Building, though not so high up. Once again, he was struck by the vividness of all the colors compared to his world.

"Quite a city, eh?" Dr. Lyst said.

"It sure is."

Telescopes were set up at strategic points so visitors could look at landmarks, interesting architecture, and historical sites. Wade put his eye up to one.

"Look that way," the doctor said, pointing. "I was born near the park. Do you see? There's a market area. Nadia's Market, we called it when I was a boy. Now they call it something else, a contrived name that's supposed to entice people to spend their money."

Wade focused the telescope until the stalls, displays, and tents became clear. He saw plenty of merchandise and food. But, apart from a few stragglers, it was surprisingly empty. "Where is everyone?" he asked.

"What do you mean?"

"I see the market and all the stalls, but there aren't any people around." Wade scanned the area. "Wait. There they are. They're crowded up at one end."

"I can guess," Dr. Lyst said.

Wade squinted to see more clearly. "They're gathered around someone. Listening to him. It's *Arin!*"

"That doesn't surprise me. He often preaches on market day."

Wade looked over at the doctor. "Preaches about what?"

"The end of the world, of course." Dr. Lyst wiggled a finger at Wade. "Would you like to see? I can show you."

Wade followed Dr. Lyst down a set of stairs and back into the laboratory. The doctor pushed a button on the wall, and a curtain moved to one side to reveal a large television. "The market, please," he said to the screen. It suddenly came to life with a full-color picture of the crowd that Wade had seen through the telescope, only the people were much closer and clearer. "Focus on the speaker, please," Dr. Lyst said. The picture moved to the right and stopped on Arin, who was gesturing at the crowd. "Sound, please," the doctor instructed.

Arin's voice suddenly boomed out. "Only in the shelter will there be protection!" he cried. "Return to the Unseen One and be saved!"

Some in the crowd laughed.

"Why should we believe you?" someone shouted.

"I don't have to give you my credentials," Arin replied. "You know me!" He moved and spoke with great energy, but he didn't sound excited. "You know that I am truthful with you. More truthful than the leaders of this city, who wish to keep the truth from you."

"Where's your golden-haired boy?" a woman asked. "Why don't you parade him out for us?"

"He's gone," Arin said.

"Gone! You mean he's vanished into thin air?" a heckler called out.

"I believe he was kidnapped."

The crowd laughed, and someone said, "Oh, that's handy!"

"Off, please," Dr. Lyst said to the television. The screen went blank.

"He's probably worried about me," Wade said thoughtfully. "I should let him know where I am."

Dr. Lyst smiled sympathetically. "I'll see that Thurston takes care of the matter."

"You think Arin is crazy, don't you?"

"Not crazy. Simply deluded." The doctor rubbed his eyes wearily. "I think anyone who feels he has to rely on some supernatural force—like the Unseen One—is trying to escape from the realities of life."

Wade wasn't sure he agreed. Arin didn't seem crazy or deluded. But what did Wade know about things like that?

"It's a lot of superstitious hocus-pocus," Dr. Lyst said.

"But what if he's right?"

"If he's right, then we'll all die as he says."

Wade shuddered. "That doesn't sound very hopeful," he replied.

"As far as I'm concerned, we're going to die anyway if we don't unite under Tyran and defeat our enemies." The doctor gazed steadily at the boy. "We each have to make a choice, Wade. We have to decide whose side we're on. You can go the way of Arin or the way of Tyran. There is no middle ground."

"I don't have to make a choice, do I? Remember, I don't belong here. Sooner or later, I'm going home. Aren't I?" Wade felt a sharp sting of panic. He imagined what it would be like if he couldn't get back. Though he enjoyed being important to Dr. Lyst and Tyran, he couldn't forget his poor mother. She'd be worried sick about him.

Dr. Lyst smiled at Wade. "As soon as we get the job done for Tyran, I'll do everything I can to get you home."

"Do you really think you'll figure out how?"

"I'll do my best. I promise."

Thurston suddenly appeared at the door. "Dr. Lyst, Tyran would like to see you," he said.

"I thought he might," Dr. Lyst replied and immediately left.

Thurston entered the room and began to look under the counters, behind a curtain, and in the corners.

"Are you looking for something?" Wade asked.

"Cromley the cat, Mr. Wade," he said. "You haven't seen him, have you?"

"No, I haven't. Is he missing?"

Thurston opened a closet door and peeked in as he explained, "He hasn't been seen since last night, which is very unusual behavior for him." He suddenly sneezed, wiped his nose with a handkerchief, then resumed his search.

"Can I help you look? I'm pretty good at finding things. At least, my mother says I am." Wade began to hunt around the lab, without success.

"Then I'm sure you are," Thurston said.

After another minute's search of the lab, Wade left with Thurston to look elsewhere for the missing cat.

CHAPTER NINE

❖————————❖

D r. Lyst knocked on the large, oak door of Tyran's study a few minutes later. He stepped in without waiting for a response, then paused. The beauty of the study always took his breath away. Windows stretched from floor to ceiling along the outside wall. Another wall was dominated by bookcases, the next wall contained paintings by some of Marus's greatest artists, and the fourth wall was fronted by more bookcases, filing cabinets, and an enormous desk behind which Tyran sat.

He was looking over some papers and spoke without looking up. "I have been watching the visual recordings of the boy on the television," he said. He poked his pen toward the large screen in the wall behind him.

"I had hoped you would," Dr. Lyst replied.

Tyran put down his pen and folded his hands under his chin. "It all sounds fanciful to me," he continued. "Is he telling you anything valuable?"

"I think his information is *very* valuable," Dr. Lyst said enthusiastically. "He's given us a whole new direction, a direction we wouldn't have thought of in our solar-based society. It's so simple … so primitive … it's little wonder we didn't think of it."

"But will it work?"

"Yes."

Tyran eyed him skeptically. "You sound awfully confident."

"Don't you see? All the elements for these bombs were right under our noses, but we didn't realize it until now. All my technicians in Hailsham have been watching our interviews on closed-circuit television. I spoke to them briefly on my way here to see you. They're already starting to put the pieces together."

"Can we create these weapons he is describing? Can we manufacture an atomic bomb?"

"I think we can. But it will take a long time."

"We do not have a long time, my friend. I have just learned that the Adrians will probably join the Albanites to fight against us. We *must* have superior weaponry to scare them off."

"If it's a scare you want to give them ..."

"Yes?"

Dr. Lyst spoke slowly, thinking aloud. "It'll take a long time to create an atomic bomb, but I think we can create some smaller yet very powerful bombs in a shorter time—they'll certainly be more powerful than the solar bombs we're throwing at each other now."

"How quickly can you produce these bombs?"

Dr. Lyst did an estimation in his head. "A month, maybe more."

"A month! We don't have a month! I must have something sooner, something *now*."

"You want the impossible."

"I *need* the impossible."

"My technicians are working around the clock."

Tyran paced with his hands clasped behind his back. "If I could stall everyone with a demonstration ... just enough to impress them that we have the capability to inflict damage ... even if we are not ready to mass-manufacture yet ... then maybe those fool elders will listen to me."

"You want to bluff them?"

"Yes. Make them think we have a whole arsenal, even if we

do not. Can you create just *one* bomb powerful enough to make them think twice about me?"

"Without testing it first—"

"Forget testing it! The demonstration will be the test!"

Dr. Lyst looked doubtful. "I can try."

"When?"

The doctor took a deep breath and closed his eyes. "Three days?"

"Make it two."

"Tyran!"

"Three days may be too late. Make it two days, my friend. I am meeting with the elders this afternoon, and I *must* have something with which to surprise them. Two days."

"Two days." Dr. Lyst sighed deeply. "I'll leave for Hailsham right away."

❖———❖

From his bedroom window, Wade watched Tyran climb into his black sedan and drive away. A moment later, Dr. Lyst left in his smaller car. Wade wondered where they were going and why Dr. Lyst had such a serious expression on his face.

Wade's attention was drawn from the window by a strange scratching sound behind the wall next to the bed. *Rats?* he wondered. But then a dark-wood panel sprang open, as if suddenly released from a latch.

Thurston stepped into the room. "Secret passageway," he said to Wade as he closed the panel behind him. "I thought Cromley had gotten in there, as he sometimes does."

Wade approached the panel and ran his finger along the almost-invisible seam. "Really? Where does it go?" he asked.

"To the various rooms, then down to an underground corridor that runs to a pump house at the edge of the gardens," Thurston replied. "I believe it was used by the servants in the old days to retrieve water."

"How does it open on this side?"

"I'll show you," Thurston said. He added cautiously, "But you mustn't go in there. It's off-limits to everyone except a few of the staff."

"Okay," Wade said.

Thurston reached up to the top-left corner of the panel, which was decorated with a small carving of a flower—just as each corner was—and pressed a petal. It released the catch, and the panel opened again.

"Cool," Wade said.

Thurston closed the panel again, then asked, "Any sign of him, sir?"

Wade turned to the room and resumed his search. "Not yet. But I haven't really looked in here yet."

He and Thurston called out, "Cromley? Are you in here?" and then looked around the room, behind the curtains, in the closets, in the bathroom, and under the furniture. In the darkest corner under the bed, Wade thought he saw something move. "I think I found him!" he called.

A few minutes later, Thurston had retrieved a lamp, and together he and Wade looked under the bed again.

"It's Cromley all right," Thurston said, then beckoned the cat.

The animal meowed weakly.

"He doesn't look very well," Wade observed.

Lying down on his back, Wade reached under the bed and, with a broad, sweeping motion, scooped up Cromley and brought him out.

Back on his feet, Wade asked, "What's wrong with him?"

Cromley looked emaciated and had a crusty, yellow substance around his nose. "I can't imagine," Thurston said. He left immediately to call a veterinarian.

❖————————❖

Tyran was ushered into the chamber of the elders and found the room virtually empty. Only Liven and Dedmon awaited him. The two men looked tired and impatient.

"Where are the rest of the elders?" Tyran asked.

"They're ill and couldn't join us today," replied Liven.

"Ill?" Tyran was skeptical.

"Yes, ill," Dedmon answered with a scowl. "You're familiar with the word, I think."

Tyran frowned. "I said I wanted to meet with *all* the elders."

"Well, you have the honor of meeting with Dedmon and myself," Liven said. "Are we not enough for you?"

"Frankly, no."

"That's too bad," Liven said and then shuffled a few of the many papers in front of him. "You'll have to make the best of it."

"This is insulting!" Tyran complained.

"Oh, please, Tyran!" Dedmon said. "We've listened to your rantings and ravings long enough." He groaned, then wiped his nose with his sleeve.

"Rantings and ravings?" Tyran asked indignantly.

Dedmon continued, "You're as bad as—what's his name? —the mad prophet."

"Arin?"

"He's the one. The two of you are cut from the same cloth."

Tyran's face turned scarlet, but he said with restraint, "You do not know what you are saying."

Liven snapped, "What's your business with us, Tyran? We have a lot to do."

"What I have to say must be said to *all* the elders."

"Well, that's clearly not possible," Dedmon said. "Speak your piece or get out."

"Dismissing me like a schoolboy, is that it?"

"Suit yourself."

Tyran fumed. "I will show you who is the master and who are the schoolboys! I have warned you."

"Yes, yes," said Dedmon with obvious boredom, "you've warned us again and again. The people will rise against us, we must unite under your rule or perish, and I'm sick of your noise. The people have *not* rallied behind you, and we have *not* perished without you. I'm so bored with indulging you."

Tyran's voice rose angrily. "See how bored you are in two days' time! You will regret speaking to me in this way!"

"I'm sure we will. But until then, if you please …" Liven gestured to the door.

"Remember this day, gentlemen, and make note of what has transpired here," Tyran threatened. Then he stormed out the door, pausing only long enough to hear the two men inside laughing at him.

CHAPTER TEN

For the rest of the day, the castle seemed to bustle with activity, but none of it involved Wade. Dr. Lyst was gone for most of the afternoon, and when he returned in the evening, he locked himself in the lab to work. Even Thurston was unavailable to Wade, since he'd taken Cromley to a veterinarian.

With time on his hands, Wade wandered the castle like a small ghost. He tried reading but found the books in Tyran's collection too political for his taste. He walked up and down the halls, glancing at the various paintings and statues, but he soon tired of that. Then he peeked in the various unoccupied rooms, strolled along the castle wall, and felt generally bored. Without Dr. Lyst, he didn't know what to do with himself.

He thought about his mother and wondered if she were upset because he'd been gone so long. It was wrong of him not to try harder to get back to his world, he figured, though he didn't have the slightest idea how to do it. Dr. Lyst had promised he would attempt to figure it out, but could he? What if *he* didn't know how? Wade then thought of Arin, who'd suggested that the Unseen One might return Wade to Odyssey. *Did Dr. Lyst remember to have Thurston tell Arin I'm all right?* he wondered.

Arin … Dr. Lyst …

They were so different. Arin believed in the doom and judgment of the Unseen One—that the end of the world was near. Dr. Lyst believed in the hope and future of Tyran—that a new beginning was at hand. And somehow Wade was the missing piece to both their beliefs. How was that possible? Wade didn't know *what* he believed.

That night, he dreamed of Arin preaching in the streets and a giant mushroom cloud growing on the horizon behind the city. The atomic bomb! Wade tried to shout, but he had no voice. Thousands died from the explosion.

The next morning, Thurston came to Wade's room as usual and threw open the curtains. Wade flinched and covered his face, as if protecting himself from an explosion.

"Are you all right, sir?" Thurston asked.

Wade was breathless. "I had a bad dream," he said.

"I'm sorry," Thurston sympathized.

Wade sat up and asked, "How's Cromley?"

Thurston turned, clasping his hands anxiously in front of him before saying, "Bad news, I'm afraid. He died last night."

"Oh, no!"

"I'm going to miss him terribly."

"Me, too," Wade said with a nod, then asked, "How did he die?"

"The veterinarian wasn't sure. He'd never seen anything like it." Thurston pulled the covers aside so Wade could get out of bed. "It's all very mysterious," he added.

Wade looked at him, perplexed.

"Not only about Cromley, but the others, I mean."

"What others?" Wade asked.

"Some of the staff have taken ill. We have only about half of our usual people in place."

"Does anybody know why?"

"No, sir," Thurston said. "Tyran called for a doctor."

Thurston went into the bathroom to start the water for Wade's bath. Wade got undressed and wrapped a robe around himself. He walked into the bathroom, where Thurston was testing the temperature of the water.

"Thurston …" Wade began hesitantly.

"Yes, sir?"

"Did Dr. Lyst ask you to deliver a message to Arin?"

"No, sir."

"Oh." Wade thought for a moment. "I'd like to go see him if you can arrange it."

"Arin?"

"Yes, please."

"I'm afraid that isn't possible," Thurston said.

"Why isn't it?"

"Tyran has given express orders not to allow anyone in or out of the castle right now."

"Why?" Wade asked in surprise.

"He and Dr. Lyst are in the middle of some very important work, and they fear that a breach of security could compromise them." Thurston stood away from the bathtub. "At least, that's what they've told me."

"In other words, he's locked us in," Wade said.

"Yes, I suppose you could put it that way."

Wade folded his arms and thought for a moment. He wanted Arin to know where he was and that he was safe. "Thurston," he said finally, "I have to get a message to Arin. I want him to know I'm all right."

"I'll see what I can do."

Wade was in the middle of his bath when it suddenly occurred to him what the "important work" was. *Dr. Lyst is making the bomb!* he thought excitedly. *He's figured out how to do it!*

Wade remembered how the atomic bomb was surrounded by top secrecy during its development. The Americans had been worried that the Germans might discover what they were up to, steal their secrets, and develop the bomb before them. Likewise, that must be why Tyran and Dr. Lyst had clamped down on security around the castle. They didn't want any of their enemies to create the bomb first. Wade felt excited and proud.

Later, during breakfast, Wade noticed how empty the castle seemed to be. Many of the staff and servants were missing, just as Thurston had said. Wade ate his toast and wondered about the illness that was going around. What kinds of germs and flus did they have in this world? Were they the same as in his?

His thinking drifted back to the atomic bomb and the effects it had on the Japanese at Hiroshima and Nagasaki. The newspapers had reported that many mysterious illnesses—some fatal—afflicted the survivors. Doctors were still trying to sort out the causes, but most agreed that the diseases were the aftereffects of the radiation from the bombs. They still had so much to learn, they said.

Radiation, Wade thought. *Does Dr. Lyst understand about the dangers of radiation?*

Wade jumped up from the table and raced to the laboratory. The doors were closed, as he expected. He knocked loudly. When no one answered, he knocked again. This time he didn't wait and opened one of the doors.

The laboratory looked empty. Then, through the doors leading to the walkway on the wall outside, he saw Dr. Lyst. The doctor was standing, looking out over the city.

"Dr. Lyst?" Wade called.

"Oh, hello, Wade," the doctor said pleasantly. He looked weary. In the distance, a ribbon of smoke rose from the city's horizon.

"What's that?" Wade asked.

"More riots."

"They're *rioting?*" Wade was concerned. "Why?"

"The war, a poor economy … it's always the same," the doctor replied. "What can they expect when they follow the fools who serve as our elders? But the moment is coming—is nearly here—when Tyran will prove himself."

Wade leaned against the wall and kept his eyes fixed on the city. "You've figured out how to build the bomb," he said as casually as he could.

Dr. Lyst sighed. "Not *the* bomb—not the atomic one—but we've come up with at least *a* bomb. A powerful one. My technicians and scientists are exhausting themselves to have it finished by tomorrow."

Wade turned to him, surprised. "Tomorrow?"

"Tomorrow," Dr. Lyst affirmed. "That's when Tyran will make his demonstration to the elders."

"That's why everyone's been so busy," Wade said.

"Yes."

From somewhere in the city, they heard a loud *crack*, like the sound of a whip snapping. It was followed by a muted scream.

"Can't the police stop it?" Wade asked.

Dr. Lyst shook his head. "They've been trying, but the people are panicked. A lot of them are sick."

"Sick from what?"

"No one is sure."

Wade waited a moment, then asked cautiously, "Did you know that a lot of people in the castle are sick, too?"

"I heard that something is going around." Dr. Lyst touched his nose. "I'm not sure I feel very well myself. But I don't have time to think about it."

"Dr. Lyst, have you been using plutonium or uranium in your research?"

Dr. Lyst turned his gaze fully to Wade. His expression was

quizzical as he answered, "We don't have such things here, but we have our own equivalent. We call it viranium. Why do you ask?"

"Because in my world, the stuff that makes the atomic bomb work is radioactive," Wade explained. "If people are exposed to it, they get sick. Sometimes they die."

"Oh, I see now. You're afraid that I've brought some of those substances to the castle and that's what's making people sick?"

"Yes. Maybe the people in the city are getting sick from it, too. See, I've been thinking about it, and maybe if you weren't careful, it might get into the water somehow."

"Don't worry about it, Wade," the doctor said, his voice full of assurance. "We have the strictest precautions in place. I have everything under control."

"Then you're not keeping any of that viranium stuff here— anywhere near the city?"

Dr. Lyst smiled. "I said not to worry. We're scientists. We're careful."

Wade wasn't sure if he believed him, but he didn't get the chance to pursue the subject because just then, Tyran appeared in the doorway between the laboratory and the castle wall. "There you are," he said. "I have been looking for you."

"Well, here I am," Dr. Lyst said, his arms outstretched as if he were presenting himself for inspection.

"You have time to stand out here and look at the view?" Tyran teased.

"I *make* time, Tyran," the doctor replied, then lectured, "As should you. You're looking very tired."

"I *am* tired," Tyran said sharply. "Tired of those idiots who call themselves our elders. They will not return any of my messages now. It was bad enough that they laughed at me yesterday, but now they are ignoring me. I will not tolerate it any longer."

"Ah! You've decided how you want to handle the demonstration?"

"Yes, providing you have good news for me."

"Good news?" Dr. Lyst nodded. "I suppose I do. Our prototype should be ready to test by tomorrow morning."

"*Should* be?" Tyran challenged him. "*Will* be, you mean."

"It *will* be."

"Excellent." Tyran rubbed his hands together briskly. "I have determined the perfect site for the demonstration."

"Where?"

"The home of one of the elders."

"A *home?*"

"Liven's mansion on the outskirts of the city."

"Not someone's home, Tyran! You can't be serious."

"I am very serious, my friend. That will show them how powerful we are, and that we mean business."

Dr. Lyst lowered his head and said softly, "No, Tyran."

"No? You are defying me, doctor?"

Dr. Lyst locked eye contact with him. "I know you're upset with the elders," he reasoned, "but murdering one of them at home is not the way."

"Murdering?" Tyran said, then suddenly laughed. "You do not understand," he explained. "I'm not out to *kill* anyone. I merely want to blow up Liven's *house*, not Liven or his family."

"That's a relief," said Dr. Lyst.

Tyran continued, "My spies have worked out Liven's routine. His wife and children are gone every morning at 10:00. His servants use that time to shop for the evening meal. The house will be empty when we do our demonstration."

"You're certain?"

"I am certain." Tyran eyed the doctor for a moment. "You are not convinced."

"I'm not convinced that blowing up anyone's house is a good idea."

"What do you think bombs are for?" Tyran said with a humorless chuckle. "Do you think Wade's country hesitated to drop those atomic bombs on their enemies just because there were *homes* in the target cities?"

"We dropped them on industrial cities," Wade said defensively.

"All the same, you destroyed homes and families. It is what happens in war."

"We're not at war with our own city," Dr. Lyst said.

"We may as well be," Tyran snapped, then turned to Wade. "Thurston asked me for permission to send a message to Arin on your behalf."

"Yes, sir. I want Arin to know that I'm with you and I'm safe."

"I told Thurston no, he did not have permission to do what you asked," Tyran said. He pushed his hands into his jacket pockets. "These are volatile times, Wade. I cannot have one of my servants seen near Arin's compound. It would give the wrong impression. Besides, why should you care whether Arin knows you are all right?"

"Because he helped me when I first arrived," Wade replied.

"Your loyalty is commendable but misguided. He would have made a spectacle of you. He only helped you because it suited his own ends."

Wade thought that statement was unfair. Arin didn't seem selfish. "And why are *you* helping me?" Wade retorted.

Tyran struck out, clipping Wade on the cheek. "Never question me in that tone again!" he ordered.

Tears sprang to Wade's eyes, more from the shock than from the blow itself. "Yes, sir," he said coldly and turned his back to Tyran to look out at the city again.

He heard Tyran march away.

Wade gently rubbed his cheek. Dr. Lyst also looked thoughtfully toward the city.

"He seems harder now, doesn't he?" Dr. Lyst said.

Wade nodded.

"He's under a lot of stress."

Wade didn't say anything.

"The demonstration will prove to the elders that it's time to listen to us. A lot is riding on its success."

Wade kept his gaze on the city.

"Things will be different after tomorrow."

Wade nodded, but he wasn't sure whether that was good or bad.

❧━━━━━━━━❧

CHAPTER ELEVEN

Now that he knew he wasn't allowed to leave the castle or get a message to Arin, Wade felt like a prisoner. "It's to keep you safe," Thurston said in the dining room, echoing the same thing Tyran had said that first night he'd arrived at the castle. Come to think of it, Arin had said the same thing about keeping Wade in the compound: It was to protect him.

Why, then, he wondered, *does being kept safe feel like being imprisoned?* He ventured to ask Thurston that question.

"Being safe and being imprisoned aren't so different," Thurston said reflectively as he picked up Wade's dinner plates. "In the hands of someone who loves you, being kept inside is safety. When you're ill, for example, your mother or father may keep you in your room so you'll get better. In the hands of someone who hates you, being kept inside is imprisonment. You're kept locked up so you'll stay out of the way or won't be able to speak or cause trouble, or to punish you."

"So who loves me?" Wade asked. "Tyran or Arin?"

Thurston smiled at him warily. "That's not for me to say," he replied.

Wade remembered how Tyran had struck him on the face earlier in the day. Was that the act of a man who loved him? Wade thought he knew the answer. It was easy to think now that all of Tyran's kind words and friendly gestures had been to get Wade to tell them about the atomic bomb. But what about Dr. Lyst? He had always acted like Wade's friend. Or was that a trick, too?

Wade felt foolish and thought again about Arin. "Stay in

the compound," Arin had said, "so no harm will come to you and you won't be used to cause harm." Wade had felt disappointed and trapped when Arin had said that. Now …

Now he had to wonder: *Is this what Arin meant? Have I been used to cause harm?*

"Will that be all, sir?" Thurston asked.

"Yes, thank you," Wade answered.

Thurston bowed slightly, and Wade noticed for the first time how pale he looked. "Are you feeling all right, Thurston?" he asked.

"Not very," he replied, then took a tray of dirty dishes to the kitchen.

That night, Wade dreamed that he had climbed to the top of the castle wall to see the city—just as he'd climbed the wall of Arin's compound. But the ladder fell and he was stuck on the wall. To his horror, he saw that the wall was rigged with explosives, and they were set to go off in two minutes. He didn't know what to do. Then a voice called to him from below. It was Arin, with outstretched arms, shouting, "Jump! I'll catch you! I'll protect you!" Wade was poised on the ledge, unable to make his decision, when the bombs went off.

Wade awakened to a dark room. Once he realized it was only a dream, he lay back and tried to calm his fast-beating heart. He rolled over to look at the small clock on the bedstand. It was after nine o'clock.

Nine o'clock at night? That didn't make sense. He had gone to bed at 10:00. Tumbling out from under the covers, he went over to the curtains and pushed them aside. A glorious morning greeted him.

"Where's Thurston?" he wondered out loud. Pulling on his robe, he went into the hallway. Everything seemed unnaturally quiet. He made his way to Dr. Lyst's laboratory and was relieved to find the doctor there. "Good morning," Wade said.

"Is it? I'm not so certain," the doctor replied, pacing around the room with great agitation. He looked pale and had dark circles under his eyes.

"I overslept," Wade explained. "Thurston didn't wake me up like he normally does. Do you know where he is?"

"What?"

"Where's Thurston?"

Dr. Lyst waved his hand impatiently. "I haven't the foggiest. Probably with the rest of the staff, finding vantage points from which to watch Tyran's demonstration."

"He's going through with it? You finished the bomb?"

"Please, Wade, don't bother me with questions now. I'm annoyed—*most* annoyed."

"What's the matter?"

"The matter?" The doctor looked at him as if he were stupid. "I was up all night at our laboratory in Hailsham, that's what's the matter. Half my scientists and technicians have come down with this blasted illness. And I had Tyran breathing down my neck the whole time."

"Did you finish your prototype of the bomb?" Wade asked.

"I wouldn't call it a prototype. A prototype means we'll make more like it, and we won't. No, sir, we won't make another one like it. It was a mess."

"You mean it won't work?"

Dr. Lyst suddenly blew his nose, then answered, "It'll work, all right. It'll blow that house to smithereens. But I wouldn't want to make another like it. We needed *time*, I kept telling Tyran. We have to test these things *carefully*. But he wouldn't listen. Oh, no, he wouldn't. He'll have his demonstration, but I won't let him pressure me like that again. I want my bombs to be *right*. It's a wonder his men weren't blown up carrying the bomb to the house."

"*His* men?"

"Why do you keep asking so many questions!" Dr. Lyst shouted. "He wouldn't let me or my technicians set the bomb up. He had his *soldiers* do it—as if they know anything about my bombs. 'You'll be spotted,' he said. 'My soldiers will creep in quietly, set the bomb, and creep away. No one will know they were there. But you and your technicians would blunder in and give the whole thing away.' Can you imagine? He said we would *blunder* in! *Blunder!* Well, if it all goes wrong, he'll have no one to blame but himself."

Wade didn't know what to say.

Dr. Lyst looked at Wade as puzzlement moved across his face like a shadow. "Why are you still in your bathrobe?"

"Thurston didn't wake me up," Wade explained again.

"For heaven's sake, get dressed, Wade! This is a big day!"

Wade rushed back to his room and hastily washed himself, watered down his hair so it wouldn't stick up at odd angles, dressed, then returned to the lab.

Dr. Lyst was out on the castle wall with a telescope. He handed Wade a large pair of powerful binoculars. "We'll see everything from here," he said, then sighed. "I hope you're pleased with your creation."

"*My* creation?"

Dr. Lyst eyed him impatiently. "Must you always speak in question marks? Yes, it's your creation as much as it's mine."

❖———✦———❖

Tyran made his demands clear in the elders' meeting. Liven and Dedmon, along with Acad, who was obviously ill, argued with him.

"You think we're going to hand the reins of power over to you simply because you *tell us* we should?" Dedmon asked. He sniffled, then blew his nose loudly.

Liven stood up to face Tyran. "We've been more than patient with you, Tyran," he said. "Leave now or I'll have my guards throw you out."

Tyran smiled and said, "Your guards are currently being subdued by *my* guards."

"What?" Liven said. He marched over to the chamber door, threw it open, and found himself face-to-face with three of Tyran's men. They scowled at him and looked all the more menacing because of their sharp, black uniforms and high jackboots. Liven turned to Tyran. "You can't do this!" he insisted. "It's treason!"

"It is only a temporary measure, to make sure we are not interrupted until my demonstration is finished," Tyran replied as if nothing were wrong.

"What demonstration?" Acad asked weakly from his chair.

Tyran looked at his watch. "The demonstration that will take place in about five minutes. But you gentlemen will have to come up to the roof with me."

"I'm not going anywhere," Acad said.

"Neither am I," Dedmon added.

"Shall I call my guards to help persuade you?" Tyran threatened.

The three elders looked to one another.

"We'll go," Liven said. "But this had better be the most remarkable thing we've ever seen."

"It will be," Tyran said. "It will be."

Tyran and the elders reached the roof in four minutes. Acad looked as if he might expire right then and there from the journey.

"Now what?" Liven asked.

"Look off to the east."

"What about it?"

"More specifically, look in the direction of the Cinemon suburbs—that wondrously large and exclusive selection of houses there," Tyran said, pointing.

"You know that's where I live," Liven said with a frown.

"By no small coincidence, it *is* where you live!" Tyran said dramatically. "That single large house over on the Cinemon Ridge—off by itself—will be the site of our demonstration. Look through the telescopes I have provided, please." He gestured to the telescopes. "Go on. Everyone have a look."

"I see my house," Liven said, flatly unimpressed.

"In five seconds you will not."

"What do you mean?"

"Watch." Tyran counted down slowly. "Five ... four ... three ..."

"Two ... one," Dr. Lyst counted down. When he reached *one*, he tensed in anticipation of the explosion. It didn't come. "Something's wrong," he said a few seconds later. "Something's gone wrong!"

"This is ridiculous!" Liven said and pushed the telescope away.

Tyran was red-faced. "Wait! It will come," he assured them.

"I don't know what you're up to," Liven said with a scowl, "but your time is up."

"No!" Tyran said.

"Let's go back to our meeting, gentlemen," Liven suggested to Dedmon and Acad.

Tyran held up his hands to stop them. "No! It will happen."

Liven pointed a finger at Tyran. "And you'd better be glad that whatever you were doing failed. Because if you do anything to hurt my family or my house or *anything that is mine*, you won't live to regret it."

Tyran turned scarlet and suddenly grabbed Liven. "You will stay here and watch until I tell you it is time to go!" he demanded. "Now watch!"

❖━━━━━━━━━❖

Dr. Lyst was talking into something that resembled a walkie-talkie, trying to learn what had gone wrong with the bomb.

Wade continued to look at Liven's house through the binoculars. It was a large, Romanesque building with pillars in the front. Tall windows lined the first and second floors.

"Well?" Dr. Lyst shouted into the communicator. "What happened?"

A garbled voice said something back to him that Wade didn't understand.

"Say that again?" Dr. Lyst commanded.

Wade scanned the house. It looked impressive in the mid-morning light. The pillars cast shadows against the white stone. The sun glinted in the windows. Suddenly, Wade froze. Something had moved in one of the windows. He was sure of it. "Dr. Lyst!" he said, his mouth going dry.

He now saw a woman clearly in one of the upper windows. She had opened it and was shaking a large cloth—maybe it was a small rug—out the window.

"Dr. Lyst," Wade cried out, "there's someone in the house!"

"There can't be. It's supposed to be empty," the doctor said and pressed his eye against the telescope lens. "Oh, no!" He lifted the communicator again and started to say, "Abort the detonation!"

Just then, the house exploded.

The brilliance of the flash made Wade wince. The sound rattled his ribcage, the windows of the castle, and the wall under his feet. Then, for a moment, a sickening silence hung over the city. No dogs barked, no birds sang, no horns sounded, and not a human being moved or breathed.

A moment later, from somewhere far below, Wade heard a baby begin to cry.

⟩————————⟨

Liven slumped to the floor of the roof. His face had gone completely white. He stared into an emptiness only he could see. One second his house was there and Sheresh, his housemaid, was shaking out a small rug from his son's bedroom window—and the next second it was all gone. The house, the road leading up to it, the trees surrounding it, and even a large chunk of the Cinemon Ridge itself—all were obliterated. Only a scorched, black smudge marked where his home had been.

"You're a madman," Acad whispered.

Tyran looked at them one by one and spat out, "You laughed at me! Well, now let me hear you laugh!"

Dedmon and Acad stared at him.

"My wife, my children," Liven said as if bringing himself out of his shock.

"They are safe," Tyran said. "Your wife is running her usual morning errands, and your children are at school."

"Sheresh was there."

"The house was empty."

"Sheresh the housemaid was there! I saw her! Right before the blast."

Tyran turned to one of his guards, who nodded quickly to confirm Liven's statement.

"If she was there," Tyran said, "she was not supposed to be."

"She's dead! You killed her!" Liven cried out. The rage contorted his face as he rushed to attack Tyran. Tyran quickly stepped out of his path. Liven stumbled and fell to the ground. He lay there, sobbing heavily.

Tyran turned to Acad and Dedmon. "You have seen the power I have," he said coldly. "My explosives will bring our enemies to their knees. Now, the question is, whose side do you want to be on? Mine or theirs?"

"What kind of deal are you offering us?" Acad asked.

"You make me the governor of this realm," Tyran said.

"You say 'governor,' but you mean 'dictator,' am I correct?" Dedmon asked.

"I am willing to allow the elders to serve as an advisory board in my new government. You will not have to lose your prestige or positions. But I expect your loyalty."

Acad wheezed for a moment, then asked, "And what if we don't agree?"

"Then perhaps *all* your homes will be destroyed as Liven's was." Tyran stared them down with cold eyes. "And next time, I may not care whether your families are still inside. Think about it."

CHAPTER TWELVE

❖————————❖

Wade barely made it to the wall before heaving the contents of his stomach over the side. It was more than his mind could take: A woman going about her business as she probably had for years on end, casually shaking a rug out a window, was dead. Did she have a husband? Children? Friends? Other loved ones? None of it mattered now. The bomb had gone off, and she was dead. And for what? So Tyran could give a demonstration.

Wade began to shake uncontrollably as the tears fell down his cheeks.

Dr. Lyst angrily threw down the communicator. It shattered into small pieces on the hard stones of the walk. Then he kicked at the telescope until it fell over. "Does he realize what he's done!" he shouted.

"He killed her," Wade said.

"Yes, he did. He killed her," Dr. Lyst said. "And it won't bode well for our cause!"

Wade wasn't sure he'd heard Dr. Lyst correctly. "Our cause?" he asked.

"We want the people to follow Tyran because he's a man of power and of vision," Dr. Lyst said, "not because they're afraid of him."

"Didn't you see what just happened, Dr. Lyst?" Wade complained. "He *killed* an innocent woman!"

Dr. Lyst waved his hand dismissively. "Oh, that. Yes, yes, it's tragic. But worse, it could damage our plans."

Wade gaped at Dr. Lyst. "You don't care, do you?" he said,

shocked by the revelation. "You don't care that she died."

"Oh, *please*, Wade," Dr. Lyst said. "I have more important things to care about than the life of a housemaid."

Suddenly, Wade remembered something Muiraq and Arin had said about the evil of this generation: The first thing to go when people turn their backs on the Unseen One is their humanity. "Men who commit heinous and immoral acts become heroes—giants in the land," Arin had said. "Lives become expendable to wicked ideals and causes. We celebrate inhumanity because we no longer understand what it is to be human."

Tyran returned to the castle within the hour. Wade followed Dr. Lyst to Tyran's office, where their leader was clearly delighted. "The elders have agreed to support me!" he announced happily. "Now I must seize the momentum and make a speech in the city square."

"Slow down," Dr. Lyst said. "I think we should have a chat."

"I do not have time," Tyran said.

Dr. Lyst persisted. "I'm afraid you're losing sight of your goals," he warned.

"What are you talking about? I am *achieving* my goals—as of this day!" He clapped Dr. Lyst on the shoulder. "And you made it possible with that wonderful bomb of yours. But you cannot waste time. We need more of them."

"Listen to me, Tyran—"

"My throat is getting raw," Tyran interrupted, deaf to Dr. Lyst's concern. "Does anyone have a lozenge?" He went to his desk to find one.

"Tyran!" Dr. Lyst snapped.

Tyran stopped where he was and looked at the doctor.

"I understood about blowing up the house," Dr. Lyst

continued. "That was a solid demonstration of power. But ..." He hesitated.

Impatiently, Wade picked up the thought. "But you killed an innocent woman this morning!" he said.

Tyran turned to Wade and said casually, "Yes ... and?"

Wade didn't know what to say. He had hoped Tyran might feel some sense of remorse. "Aren't you sorry?" he finally asked.

Tyran's gaze went from Wade to Dr. Lyst. "Why is this boy bothering me with stupid questions?" he asked.

Dr. Lyst took another tack. "Whether you're sorry or not, the crowds may not be, shall we say, *appreciative* that you killed one of their own," he suggested. "She was a *worker*, Tyran. You're supposed to be representing the workers, not killing them."

"Why should I care what the crowds think? The destruction of that house—and her death—demonstrated that I mean business. They will strike fear into their hearts."

"Destruction? Death? Fear?" Dr. Lyst lashed out. "Is that what you're after now? I thought it was *vision* and *strength* and *freedom*."

"Sometimes the only way to persuade the people toward things like vision, strength, and freedom is to scare them."

"No. In the long run, fear only leads to more fear, and then to oppression."

"I am losing my patience, doctor. I have an important speech to make, and I do not need you to muddle my thinking. Now, I suggest you and the boy get dressed for our big moment."

"You want *us* to go with you?" Wade asked.

"Yes. You will be on the grandstand with me. I want the people to see the brains behind my bombs and"—he gestured to Wade—"the *inspiration* behind them. Now *hurry*."

"But—" Wade started to argue, but Dr. Lyst signaled him to be quiet. It was time to leave.

When they were out of Tyran's earshot, Dr. Lyst said, "There's no talking to him when he gets like that."

"What are we going to do?" Wade asked.

"I don't know. I'm afraid he's lost control."

"I don't want to go to his speech. I don't want anyone to think I'm with him."

Dr. Lyst glanced at Wade. "But you *are* with him," he observed.

"Not anymore," Wade said. "Not after he killed that woman."

"I'm afraid you have no choice."

✦————✦

Thurston was nowhere to be found, so Wade had to rummage around for clothes to wear. In a spirit of defiance, he decided to wear the clothes Arin had given him after he'd first arrived: light trousers and tunic with a robe. The outfit seemed just right for the warm, sunny day.

Wade considered trying to escape. He didn't like the idea of being on display at Tyran's speech. And the more he thought about it, the sicker he felt for his part in blowing up the house and killing the poor servant woman. *If I hadn't talked to them about the atomic bomb, it might not have happened,* he told himself. He looked over at the wall panel next to the bed, the one that led to the secret passageway. *Maybe I can escape through there.*

Before he could decide, however, a stern-looking guard came to the room and indicated that Wade should follow him.

They walked down the main hall to the courtyard, where Tyran and Dr. Lyst were waiting. A flicker of surprise showed in Tyran's eyes when he recognized Wade's clothes. "Nice outfit," he said sarcastically. Then he motioned for everyone to get into the back of his black sedan, and they drove into Sarum.

Wade was startled to see the condition of the city. The windows in many shops and homes were shattered, more so as they drove to the center square.

"Did the rioters break them?" Wade asked.

"Maybe some, but most of the damage was caused by the explosion," Dr. Lyst explained. "It was a far more powerful bomb than even I suspected."

"Yes, it was," Tyran affirmed with a smile.

Wade also noticed that many of the shops were closed. "Is it a holiday?" he asked.

"It will be after today," Tyran said. "We will call it 'Independence Day.'"

Dr. Lyst ignored him and said, "A lot of the people are sick with this mysterious illness that's going around. The hospitals are packed with patients. The city health authorities are now calling it an epidemic."

"One more thing for me to blame on the elders," Tyran said.

"*You'll* find a cure for it?" Dr. Lyst asked skeptically.

"No," Tyran replied. "As my leading scientist, *you* will find a cure for it."

Wade was tempted to bring up the subject of the effects of radiation, but he thought Dr. Lyst might get angry with him. He decided to remind the doctor of it later, in private.

As they approached the town square, the crowds thickened. People milled around aimlessly, though some had picket signs protesting the morning's explosion.

Tyran instructed an aide in the front of the car, "Make a note of who the protesters are. We will deal with them later."

The aide nodded and lifted a communicator to his mouth. "Photograph and identify the protesters," he ordered someone on the other end.

The car made its way slowly through the hordes of people who were gathering for Tyran's speech. Many stopped to watch the black sedan drive past. Wade was struck by how pale and tired everyone looked. One man stumbled against the car, and Wade nearly cried out. The man had a sickly, yellow crust oozing from his nose. *Just like Cromley*, Wade thought.

Wade glanced at Dr. Lyst. The doctor shook his head as if to warn Wade not to say anything.

The car came to a halt, and guards gathered around the doors so Tyran, Dr. Lyst, and Wade could have safe passage to the large grandstand set up at the back of the square. Some of the people applauded as the three of them walked up the stairs. A few hecklers booed them, but they were instantly silenced by other members of the crowd.

Wade heard someone mention his blond hair. Then an old woman pointed at him and shrieked, "He's the one! He's the cause of our problems!"

"Ignore her," Dr. Lyst said as they sat down in chairs behind the podium.

Wade shifted uncomfortably in his seat. Hundreds and hundreds of people were crushed into the square, and they all seemed to be looking at him. He didn't like the attention. He wondered, also, if they would truly be angry about the death of the housemaid.

Tyran approached the podium and lightly tapped a stick-like object attached to the top. The tapping was amplified from speakers stationed all around the square. It was a thin microphone, Wade realized. It wasn't like the fat, oblong microphones used for radio and television speeches back in his world.

"Ladies and gentlemen, your attention, please," Tyran said, his voice booming throughout the square. The crowd quieted down. "This is the dawning of a new day for Sarum—and for the entire nation. Many of you witnessed that dawning in the power of the explosion that rocked our city this morning."

A hum of discussion worked its way through the crowd.

Tyran continued, "I confess to you that it was the house of Liven, our foremost elder, which was destroyed."

The hum of discussion grew louder.

"I confess to you that, sadly, his housekeeper was killed in the explosion."

The crowd grew louder still.

"I also confess to you that I, Tyran, was responsible for the explosion."

Now the crowd erupted in a cacophony of shouts and cries.

Here it comes, Wade thought as he braced himself. *They'll riot now.*

But the shouts and cries weren't in protest, he quickly realized. They were calling out things like "How?" and "Where did you get this power?" and "Tyran's a genius!"

Wade couldn't believe what he was hearing. They weren't angry or rebellious; they were *impressed.*

A handful of people off to one side yelled, "You murdered an innocent woman!" but they were shouted down by the majority of the crowd. Wade thought he saw some of Tyran's guards move in to arrest them.

Tyran turned to Dr. Lyst and Wade and winked at them. He went on, "We have developed this power through the genius of Dr. Lyst, whom many of you know, and through a young stranger who was sent to us by fate!" Tyran waved his hand toward Dr. Lyst and Wade.

The crowd began to applaud. The sound moved like a wave toward the stage. Then came the cheers and shouts. Tyran gestured for Wade and Dr. Lyst to stand up. The doctor obeyed. When Wade didn't move from his seat, the doctor reached over and pulled him to his feet. Wade blushed and wished the stage would collapse and swallow him right then. *They don't care*, he thought as the people cheered for a full five minutes. Wade thought of Arin again and all he'd said about the wickedness of this generation.

"The power you saw this morning was to prove the validity of my claims to leadership," Tyran said when the crowd had calmed down again and Wade and Dr. Lyst had retaken their seats. "You know well the work I have been trying to accomplish in this city on your behalf. You know well how I have fought for your rights and your prosperity. You know well how I have been thwarted time and again by the elders, who are more concerned about their own reputations and pockets than about the people of this city. Have they not allowed us to be attacked on all sides by our enemies? Have they not allowed a mysterious illness to run rampant throughout the city?"

At this the crowd began to shout and cheer again.

Tyran waved at them to quiet down. "Those days are over!" he continued. "They have seen the power that I warned them I have harnessed and have agreed to make me the *governor of Marus*."

The crowd howled and applauded.

"The days of privilege for the few are over. From this day forward, I will lead this nation into a new era, an era of prosperity and of victory over the many enemies who threaten us!"

The people seemed uncontrollable in their enthusiasm.

"Let them be warned!" Tyran cried out. "Let them all quiver in the face of our power! We, the people of Marus, are rising from the ashes to victory!"

The crowd responded with a deafening roar. Tyran basked in their approval for a moment, then waved them once more to silence.

"If you are with me—if you swear allegiance to my cause—then I swear allegiance to you," Tyran said. "Let us all bow and pledge ourselves to a united city, a united nation, and a united future together!"

Slowly, the crowd began to kneel. Tyran took the microphone from the stand and also knelt there on the stage. Dr. Lyst slid from his seat to his knees. Wade watched them with an ache in his heart. The doctor reached over and tugged at Wade's robe. Wade looked at him. He gestured for Wade to kneel. Wade shook his head. Dr. Lyst frowned at him and gestured more firmly. Wade whispered, "No. We don't kneel to leaders in our world."

"But you're in *this* world now," Dr. Lyst whispered back. "And I strongly urge you to kneel now."

Wade was suddenly aware that the audience had noticed his hesitation. Tyran looked at him from the corner of his eye, then hooked a thumb at one of his guards at the edge of the stage. The guard moved slowly toward the stairs. Wade had no doubt that he would be made to kneel whether he wanted to or not.

"You're only supposed to kneel to God," Wade said quickly, as if it would make a difference to anyone. It didn't. But Wade was now stubbornly determined to keep his seat. *Kneeling to Tyran would be like worshiping him,* Wade thought. *I won't do it.*

The crowd was silent. The only sound Wade heard was the guard's footsteps on the stairs leading to the stage. Wade glanced around, a panic growing in his gut. He would make a run for it if he had to.

The guard was only a few feet away when a voice cried out from the crowd, "Don't touch the boy!"

All eyes went to the source of the voice. A single man stood in the center of the kneeling crowd. It was Arin.

CHAPTER THIRTEEN

"Is this what it's come to?" Arin shouted defiantly, his voice in no need of amplification. "Now you're kneeling to a man because he makes a few promises? Because he can destroy houses? Because he murders innocent people?"

"Go back to your compound, Arin!" someone yelled at him. "You have no place here."

Tyran stood up. "No," he beseeched the crowd, "I am glad the prophet is here."

Arin smiled. "Are you?" he challenged. "Will you try to bully me into kneeling just like you were going to bully the boy?"

"I am glad you are here," Tyran said, "because the dawn of our new age would not be complete without saying farewell to the old age. *You* are that old age."

"You will say good-bye to this age—and this world!" Arin said, pointing at Tyran. "Hear the words of the Unseen One: 'The stench of your wickedness has filled My nostrils, just as the stench of your dying bodies will fill the nostrils of the vultures who will feast on you!'"

"You preach doom, Arin, and the people of this city are tired of it," Tyran countered. "I promise that the next house to be destroyed will be your own. I will see to it personally."

"You will see to nothing, for your eyes will be filled with the disease of your sin."

"Witness for yourselves!" Tyran said to the crowd. "I bring you a promise of a new beginning, a new era, and Arin whines of doom and disease. Have we not all suffered enough from his words?"

The crowd began to rise. "Yes!" one man shouted. This affirmation was followed by more.

"Away with Arin!" someone else cried out. It soon became a chant that they shouted as one voice: "Away with Arin! Away with Arin!"

"As your new governor, I will make Arin my first case of judgment!" Tyran said. "I will show him how well our city tolerates his madness! Bring him to me!"

The crowd, now a mob, turned on Arin, reaching for him. Wade jumped to his feet, desperate to see what would happen next. At first he thought Arin might fight back—he raised his arms as if to swing out against them—but then he suddenly dropped down, as if falling to his knees. The crowd moved in to the center, but it soon became obvious that the people were confused. The men and women looked around helplessly. "Where is he?" many shouted.

Arin was gone.

Men dressed similarly to Arin were suddenly grabbed and beaten by mistake. This triggered more confusion and violence. In no time at all, the rally had turned into a riot. Tyran shouted for control, but no one listened.

The old woman who had yelled at Wade before now leaped to the stage. "Seize the boy!" she shrieked. "He is evil!"

Tyran's guards tried to grab her and the other people who also climbed onto the stage, but they were outnumbered. Dr. Lyst suddenly stepped between Wade and the oncoming swarm, pushing Wade backward. Wade stumbled to the rear edge of the stage. "Run!" Dr. Lyst shouted at him.

Wade saw a gap between the back of the stage and the wall of the building next to which it had been assembled. He wiggled down through the gap and found himself in the hollow underside of the grandstand. It was an empty catacomb of wooden crossbeams, completely enclosed from the crowds beyond. The mob's footsteps sounded like thunder above.

Wade half-ran, half-crawled in a hunched-over position away from the noise. He ducked and dodged the woodwork and finally reached the end of the grandstand. Squeezing through another gap, he found himself in the open again, but at the far rear corner of the stage. Most of the mob was still around to the front. He crouched low, hoping no one would see him. He heard a child scream. Startled, he turned to see that the child was screaming at *him*. He raced down an alley away from the square. Behind him, someone cried, "There he goes!"

The alley led to another alley, which in turn deposited him onto a main street. Wade slowed to a trot and tried to blend in, but the people soon noticed his blond hair and reacted with fear. Some tried to grab him once they realized he was being pursued by the crowd behind. He legged it down another alley, this one darker, with garbage littered along the walls and tattered clothes hanging from laundry lines above. He ducked into a doorway and started to tie the collar of his robe over his head to hide his hair. A pursuer reached the opening to the alley and said, "I think he went this way!"

Wade panicked and reached behind him. His fingers wrapped around a door latch, and he pushed on it. The door opened easily. Wade slipped in, closing the door behind him as quietly as he could. Breathlessly he waited. The mob rushed by with the sound of an angry lion, kicking garbage cans and tearing at the hanging clothes on the way.

Wade didn't know how he knew, but he suddenly sensed he wasn't alone. He turned to face the room he'd just entered. It was in deep shadows except for thin shafts of light that broke through old shutters. "Is someone there?" he asked.

A raspy whisper replied, "What are you doing in my house?"

"I'm sorry," Wade said. "Those people were chasing me, and—"

"Are you a thief?" asked the whisper.

"No."

"Come closer."

Wade squinted, hoping to see what he was supposed to get closer to. As his eyes adjusted, he made out a bed in the corner of the room. The whisperer was in it. Wade slowly made his way over.

"Take that cloth off your head," the whisper ordered.

Reluctantly, Wade obeyed.

The whisper chuckled, then broke into a harsh cough. "I thought so," it said eventually. "Don't you know me?"

Wade looked closer and was repulsed by what he saw. The gaunt face looked as if someone had draped a thin layer of skin on a skull. A mustache hung limply above the upper lip. Crusty, yellow patches gathered around the nose and the corners of the eyes. Yet Wade knew the face.

"You were one of the men who kidnapped me," Wade observed.

"Movan at your service," the whisper replied.

"What happened to you?"

The face turned away for a moment to cough, then said, "I got sick. Can't imagine what it is, but I'm having a hard time shaking it. I'm sure I will, though. Just a few days' rest and I'll be back on my feet."

"You should see a doctor," Wade suggested.

"I already did. He told me to go to the hospital. I hate hospitals. They take you in the front door, then send you to the cemetery out the back. Not for me, thanks. I'll take my chances here in the comfort of my own bed." Movan wheezed for a moment. "So they're giving you a run for your money?"

"Sort of."

"You can lay low here for a while. I don't mind, if you don't mind making me some tea." The lips stretched across the teeth in a stark grin. The mustache drooped more.

Wade shuffled uncomfortably. "The crowd is gone. I should go."

"Tell you what: Stay here and I'll pretend to hold you hostage. Then we'll split the ransom money from the highest bidder. How about that?"

"No, thank you."

"Just a thought."

Wade moved slowly toward the door. "Good-bye, Movan," he said. "I hope you get better soon."

"I hope so, too. Maybe I'll see you around."

"Maybe." Wade carefully opened the door, checked the alley in both directions, then stepped out. He took a deep breath to try to recover from the sight of Movan. *He isn't going to live,* Wade thought. Wade was also sure that the radioactivity from Dr. Lyst's experiments with the bombs must have gotten into the water or the air or *something* that had reached the people. That's why so many were getting sick. Tyran's castle was probably saturated with the stuff, which is why Cromley died.

But why aren't I sick? he asked himself.

No answer was forthcoming, so Wade covered his head again and walked down the alley, making sure to go away from where the crowd had run. He approached the main avenue again and, staying close to the wall, inched around the corner.

Just then, a heavy hand fell on his shoulder.

CHAPTER FOURTEEN

❖———————❖

"Don't move," Arin said quietly. He had a hood pulled over his head to shadow his features. "You move too quickly, you see. It arouses suspicion. But if you walk slowly and purposefully, people don't notice you."

"How did you escape the mob?" Wade asked.

"I am under the protection of the Unseen One. They couldn't harm me." He then said wryly, "Well, they couldn't harm me very much."

"What are we supposed to do now?"

"I would suggest we return to the compound," Arin said. "At least that's where *I'm* going. Will you come with me?"

Wade nodded, grateful for the offer.

"Come along then."

They strolled down the thoroughfare as if they didn't have a care in the world. And, as Arin had said, no one seemed to notice them.

"Now you see our world as it truly is," Arin said. "The innocent are sacrificed to the whims of wicked men. Even those who feign goodness are corrupt to the very center of their hearts. The people do not cry out with indignation or anger against evil. Now they join in, so long as it suits their own selfish ends."

"Is it really so hopeless?"

"I'm afraid it is, son. Oh, you'll find glimmers of what once was—a noble deed, a moment of self-sacrifice—but they are quickly snuffed out."

"I feel like an idiot!" Wade exclaimed. He still felt responsible for a lot of what had happened. "All I wanted to do was see the city," he said, then went on to explain how he'd climbed the wall and been lured down by Movan and Simpson, taken to the elders, and then delivered to Tyran. He concluded by saying, "Tyran tricked me."

Arin stopped and turned to face him. "Did you not climb onto the wall after I had said to stay within the compound?" he challenged.

"Yes, sir."

"Did I not warn you that everyone outside the compound was infected with evil?"

"Yes, sir."

"Then let's be clear about this: If you were tricked, you *allowed* yourself to be tricked. Correct?"

Wade hung his head and admitted, "I allowed myself to be tricked."

Arin gazed at him, but even under the shadow of his hood, Wade could see that his face wasn't stern. He looked sad and said softly, "It's the way of man—to be seduced to a place of power, a shelter of delusion. From there you can't see things as they really are. You see things only as you *want* to see them. But the Unseen One takes us to a place of humility, a shelter of grace. It's uncomfortable for us, mostly because we then see things as *He* sees them, which means we see them as they really are."

"You mean Tyran's castle versus your compound?"

"I mean your *heart*, Wade."

"I don't understand."

Arin nudged him to continue walking. "You will eventually."

As they approached the front gates of the compound, it was clear they couldn't get in that way. A mob of wild-eyed men and women was attacking it with rocks, bottles, and anything else the people could get their hands on.

"This way," Arin instructed. Wade followed him down a side alley and around to a pathway that led into one of the abandoned warehouses Wade had seen before. Arin produced a key for the tall, riveted door. He opened it, and they went inside. The warehouse was empty except for a few pallets and boxes. Arin pushed his hood back from his head. Wade took the cue and undid his makeshift hat.

They walked over to an elevator and got in, and Arin pressed the button to go down. Several floors below—Wade lost count of how many—the doors opened to a dimly lit corridor. Arin led the way, and after a few minutes they came to a long, metal staircase that reached up into blackness. Wade stayed close behind Arin, clinging to the handrail, as they went up and still farther up. Lights seemed to turn on and off as they passed, always just enough to show them the way in front.

Finally they reached another door, which Arin opened with a second key. They stepped through into the sunlight and beauty of Arin's compound. Wade looked back and saw that the door was part of what appeared to be a small toolshed.

"A secret tunnel," Wade observed. "I heard that Tyran's castle has one of these."

Arin replied with a slight smile, "All the best places have them."

Back in the house, where the noises of the mob became merely a background irritation, Wade was reunited with the rest of Arin's family. Muiraq doted on him and gently chastised him for disappearing the way he had. Arin announced that there would be no discussion on that subject since they all had work to do.

"The end is coming now," he said simply.

"*Now?*" Wade asked, shocked.

"Within the next few days, yes."

"How do you know?"

Arin waved his hand toward a set of newspapers scattered on the table. They were filled with headlines like "Epidemic Takes Over City!" "Health Authorities in Crisis!" and "Death Watch Begins: Illness Is Fatal for Some."

Wade read the headlines and thought again of his theory about the radiation. "I think I know what's causing this," he said. "Tyran has been working on bombs with the same kinds of ingredients we use in my world for the atomic bomb. They're radioactive. Somehow he's storing it in a place that's reaching the people. That's why they're sick."

"An explanation isn't necessary," Arin said. "The judgment of the Unseen One has come."

"But it doesn't have to! Not now!" Wade exclaimed. "Don't you see? If we can find out where Tyran is storing the radioactive stuff, we can get rid of it and save everyone. He may have some of it at the castle. But I think most of it is . . . ." Wade looked around. "Do you have a map?"

"It's no use, Wade," Muiraq said, trying to calm the boy. "It's time."

"Maybe it isn't. Maybe you're wrong," Wade insisted. Riv handed him a map of Marus. Wade found Sarum, then found Hailsham. "Here. I heard Dr. Lyst say he has a laboratory in Hailsham where they developed the bomb they used on Liven's house. It's not very far away." Wade's eye scanned the area between Hailsham and Sarum. He found what he was looking for: a river that flowed between the two of them. "In which direction does this river flow?"

Riv looked at the map. "From Hailsham to Sarum," he answered.

Wade tapped the map with his finger and explained,

"That's probably it! I'll bet the water has something radioactive in it, and that's what's making the people sick."

"Bet? This is a wager to you?" Arin said sternly. "You don't understand, Wade. The judgment of the Unseen One is here. You can't stop it no matter what you think is its source."

"But we *can*," Wade insisted. "We can tell the people not to drink the water! We can go to Hailsham and find out where the radioactivity is coming from! There are lots of things we can do! We don't have to give up!" He was shouting now.

Arin and his family watched Wade quietly. Then Arin said in a gentle tone, "You feel responsible, and you want to do something to stop this."

Wade choked back tears. "Yes," he answered simply.

"And if I tell you it's impossible, that there's nothing you can do, you won't believe me, will you?"

Wade shrugged. "I don't know what to believe."

Arin glanced at his wife, then sighed and announced to Wade, "I have brought you here for nothing. You weren't ready to come."

Muiraq put her hand on Arin's arm. "You're not letting him go back out there?" she asked.

"I can't stop him. The Unseen One wouldn't have me keep him here against his will."

Wade stammered, "I wasn't thinking *I* should go out again. Can't we call somebody? Tell the authorities?"

"We could, but who would listen to us? Anyone connected to this compound is without a voice in the city."

"And I doubt that Tyran would listen—or allow anyone to interfere with his bomb making," Oshan added.

"Dr. Lyst would listen," Wade said. "He's in charge of the bombs. He would understand."

"Dr. Lyst is in Tyran's pocket," Pool said.

"No," Wade responded. "He doesn't agree with everything Tyran's doing. We could persuade him to take action."

"*You*—not us," Arin said.

"I have to try."

"I promise you, son," said Arin gravely, "you will not alter these events by a single fraction."

Wade was resolved now. "Maybe you're right," he admitted, "but I'd feel awful for the rest of my life if I didn't try."

"Then try. And when your heart is ready, try to come back to us. This is the only place where you'll be safe."

Arin let Wade use a communicator, not unlike a telephone. He told an operator who sounded like a robot to connect him to Tyran's castle. The request caused some confusion since there was no listing for a "Tyran's castle," but eventually things got sorted out and Wade heard a rapid series of tones. He found himself talking to some kind of automatic switchboard, which put him through a series of questions, requests for passwords, and identification after he'd asked for Dr. Lyst. Finally he said angrily, "If you tell him it's Wade Mullens, he'll want to talk to me!"

The line seemed to go dead. Wade was just about to hang up when suddenly Dr. Lyst's voice crackled to life.

"Wade? Wade!" Dr. Lyst said.

"Hello, Dr. Lyst," Wade replied.

"Are you safe?" Dr. Lyst asked. "I've been worried about you."

"I'm safe. Where are you? In the laboratory?"

"No, I'm in my car, searching the streets for you." He paused to cough violently, then continued, "Tell me where you are and I'll come get you."

"Wait a minute," Wade said, then cupped his hand over the communicator. He told Arin, "He wants to know where I am."

"Tell him to meet you in front of the Dome," Arin instructed.

"The Dome?"

"He'll know where it is."

"I'll meet you in front of the Dome," Wade said into the communicator.

"Right," the doctor said. "Oh, and cover your head. There are people out here who'd like to see you dead." He hung up.

Arin led Wade back the way they'd come, through the corridor to the warehouse and back into the alley. He then guided him through the city streets until they came to a large courtyard with a building shaped like a dome in the center.

"It's a museum," Arin explained. "It was once filled with great works of art dedicated to the Unseen One. Now it's filled with the chronicles of man's folly."

"Thank you for bringing me," Wade said.

"My heart's desire is for your safety."

"I know. I'm grateful."

"Are you certain you want to go through with this? I don't trust Tyran or his Dr. Lyst."

"I don't trust Tyran either, but I think Dr. Lyst will watch out for me."

"I hope you're right." Arin glanced around and said sorrowfully, "From this moment on, the people of Sarum will not see or hear from me. My duty is fulfilled. My family and I will finish what's left to do in the shelter and go in until the Unseen One tells us it's safe to come out."

"Even if we can stop the illness?"

Arin looked as if he felt sorry for Wade. "You won't stop it any more than you can stop the turning of the tide or the rising of the two moons," he said gravely. "Look to the Unseen One, Wade, and return to us if you can."

"I will."

Wade looked over at the large front steps leading up to the Dome's entrance. He recognized Dr. Lyst's car waiting at the bottom. "There he is," Wade said. But when he turned back, Arin had disappeared.

How does he do that? Wade wondered. He walked over to Dr. Lyst's car. The door opened just as he reached it. But it wasn't Dr. Lyst inside; it was one of Tyran's guards. Wade backed away and into another guard, who quickly grabbed his arms.

"Into the car, young man!" the guard ordered. "Tyran and the doctor have been waiting for you."

CHAPTER FIFTEEN

✦———————✦

Tyran blew his nose and then pondered Wade, who was slumped in a large chair in front of Tyran's desk. Wade wondered where Dr. Lyst was.

"You were at Arin's compound," Tyran said with a hint of accusation in his tone.

"Yes, I was. How did you know that?" Wade asked.

"Dr. Lyst's communicator identified it when you called. What did Arin want with you?"

"He took me to the compound to keep me safe from the crowds."

Tyran smiled. "We will have to thank him for that one day in the future."

"He says there won't be a future. He says the end is coming now, through the mysterious illness."

"That is predictable." Tyran leaned forward against his desk. "But I do not understand. You were safe with him. Why did you make contact with Dr. Lyst?"

"Because I think I know what the illness is that's going around."

"Oh? Please enlighten me."

"First I have to go to Hailsham."

"Hailsham? Why?"

"I think the illness is a reaction to the radioactivity from your bomb experiments."

Tyran thought about it a moment, then encouraged Wade, "Go on."

"Dr. Lyst told me about the viranium he's using. If it's like our uranium or plutonium, it's radioactive. That's what's making everyone sick."

"Fascinating."

Wade sat up in his seat. "Dr. Lyst has some of the viranium here at the castle, doesn't he?"

"Yes, we have a small amount in a storage area. He has needed it for tests in his laboratory. He assured me that there was no health risk involved."

"He was wrong."

"How do you know?"

"Because Cromley died."

"Cromley—the *cat?*" Tyran laughed unbelievingly. "You will have to come up with a better example than that, my boy."

"The staff have been sick, too."

"That does not mean the viranium is causing it."

"Then let me go to Hailsham to see if the viranium has somehow gotten into the water supply. Maybe it's contaminating the river that comes to this city."

Tyran placed a hand on his chin thoughtfully. "Our laboratory *is* positioned on the river, now that you mention it," he admitted.

"Then please let me and Dr. Lyst go to check it out."

"I am not sure we can do that."

"Why not?" Wade asked, then added as an enticement, "You'll be made a hero if you can stop the illness."

Tyran looked at him skeptically. "Is that what is important to you now, making me look like a hero?"

"No," Wade replied honestly. "Stopping the sickness is what's important to me."

"Why? You do not belong here. You do not even appear to be sick. Why should you care?"

"Because ..." Wade hesitated. He didn't want to confess

the truth to Tyran, but he felt as if he had no choice. "Because I think some of this is my fault, and I want to try and make it right."

Tyran said soothingly, "You are not to blame for anything, Wade. Just the opposite. You have helped me to usher in a new age."

"I know," Wade said in a way that couldn't be mistaken. He blamed himself for Tyran's success.

"You do not like me anymore, do you?" Tyran asked.

"No."

"Why not?"

"I think you're going crazy with your power."

Tyran looked impressed. "That is interesting," he said. "Dr. Lyst made the same comment."

"He did?"

"Right after the riots. He told me to my face that he thought I was losing my grasp on reality."

"He's right."

"On the contrary, he is terribly wrong. And he is suffering for it even now."

"Suffering!"

"I do not take kindly to traitors, Wade." Tyran pushed a button on his desk. "But the two of you are too valuable for me to dispense with. So here is what I am going to do: I am going to put you in my own personal prison in the tower. That will give you a chance to think things over. It is not too late to prove your allegiance."

Guards suddenly appeared on both sides of Wade's chair. He stood up, and they led him to the door.

"Wade," Tyran said before they left the room, "your refusal to kneel was deeply humiliating to me. Even though I suspect you have more information that would be of use to me, a part of me regrets that you were not killed in the riots. Your martyrdom would have brought more sympathy to my cause. Now we will have to come up with other plans for you."

The guards took Wade away.

✦━━━━━━━━━✦

The tower was exactly that: a tower on one side of the castle, with a long, narrow staircase leading to the top. At various landings were doors leading to small cells, each containing a straw mattress on a wooden frame, an old blanket, a wooden table, and a bucket to use as a toilet. Each cell also had a narrow slit in the wall that had once been used by archers to fight off enemies. It was called an arrow loop, Wade remembered reading in a history book. When they got to his cell at the top of the tower, Wade looked out and took in the entire city of Sarum. But the view was small consolation for his loss of freedom.

The door slammed behind him, and the key grated in the lock.

What am I going to do now? he wondered. *And what's happened to Dr. Lyst?*

He hoped the doctor would find out where he was and come rescue him. But what if he wasn't able? What if Tyran had tortured or killed him? Sinking into despair, Wade lay down on the mattress. Within seconds, he felt fleas biting at him. He leaped up, slapping his skin. When he thought he had killed them all, he grabbed the blanket, beat it against the wall, then sat on it away from the bed. There he remained as the sun faded and night claimed the sky.

He couldn't sleep. The cell was cool and damp and made his bones ache. He paced around the room to keep from getting stiff. Somewhere outside, he thought he heard women crying.

Occasionally something exploded and he wondered if the city were being attacked by planes again. Peeking through the arrow loop, he saw bright reds, greens, golds, and silvers erupting in the sky. Fireworks?

He jumped when he heard a key in the door.

"Stand back from the door!" a man shouted.

Wade watched from his place by the arrow loop as the door opened and a guard entered. He was an older man with white hair and a face drawn into a permanent frown. He wore a shabby version of Tyran's guards' uniforms—the smart black had faded to a dull gray, and the shiny jackboots were scuffed and worn. The guard sniffled and, without saying a word, dropped a tray of food onto the small table. He then turned to leave again.

"Excuse me," Wade said.

"What do you want?" the guard snarled.

"My bed is full of fleas."

"So what?"

"Don't you have something I can use to kill them?"

"What's wrong with your hands?"

"I mean, a powder or something like that."

The guard shrugged. "I'll ask."

"Oh, and—"

"What?" the guard asked impatiently. He suddenly and violently sneezed into his hands and wiped them on his trousers. "Well?"

"I was wondering about the fireworks. Is a celebration going on?"

"Tyran has negotiated treaties with the Albanites and the Palatians. They won't be attacking anymore. The Adrians, Monrovians, and Gotthardites are expected to agree to a peace as well. Any more questions, your highness?"

"When can I leave here?"

"When Tyran says." The guard went to the door.

"Will you please tell Dr. Lyst that I'm up here? He may want to talk to me."

"Dr. Lyst is in no condition to talk to you."

"Why not?" Wade asked.

"He's sick. I think he caught what a lot of the rest of us have."

"Oh, no …"

"But I'll tell him if I see him, which won't be likely."

"Thank you."

"Good night."

"You'll be back in the morning?"

"Maybe."

The guard left, slamming the door and locking it again.

Wade looked down at the tray of food. It contained a bowl of a murky, brown broth, a piece of bread, and a cup of water. He sat down, slowly dipped the bread into the broth, and began to cry.

❖————————❖

Wade had curled up under the blanket next to the wall, but he hardly slept. The guard returned the next morning with another bowl of brown broth, bread, and water. Wade asked him about the flea powder, but the guard merely grunted. "I don't feel very good," he complained. "I haven't had time to ask."

The guard certainly didn't look good. His face was pallid. His eyes were bloodshot, and his nose was red and raw from wiping it. He coughed with a deep-chested raspiness.

"Is the sickness still spreading in the city?" Wade asked.

"Yes. Everyone seems to have it."

"Have the doctors found a cure?"

"Doctors!" he snorted. "They're useless. People are dying left, right, and center, and the doctors can't do a thing about it."

Wade was shocked. "People are *dying*?"

The guard's expression told Wade that he didn't want to talk about this anymore. "I'll be back at lunchtime," he said with a tone of finality. He left again.

Wade listened for the click of the lock. He then went to the door and looked it over carefully. It was made of solid wood, with the hinges on the hall side. The lock was basic: The key turned the bolt into the frame. Wade peeked into the lock itself and could see the dark hallway beyond. The guard obviously took the key with him.

Wade sat down to his breakfast. The brown broth turned his stomach, so he pushed it away. He absentmindedly chewed on the bread. What was he going to do? How long would Tyran keep him locked up? Was this a quick punishment for his rebellion, like being sent to his room, or a long-term sentence?

The morning dragged on slowly. Wade took to pacing from one end of the room to the other, which wasn't far at all. His mind raced with all the events that had brought him to this point. He thought of Arin and his family, of the compound that Arin had said was the birthplace of this world, and of the Unseen One. Arin was so certain about his faith in this person no one could see; he was convinced of the reality of the message he'd spent most of his life proclaiming. "Repent!" Arin had said again and again to those who wouldn't listen. And now he stood alone—just he and his family—sure that the end was imminent. *What if it is?* Wade mused. *What if the end comes and I'm still trapped here? Will I die here?*

Wade kicked at the table leg. This was all his fault. He was so quick to ignore Arin and so ready to believe in Tyran and Dr. Lyst. Why? Little wonder, really. Tyran and Dr. Lyst made him feel important; they appreciated him for all the things he got teased about at school; they made him think he was part of a glorious new day in this strange world. Arin, on the other hand, told him he was a sign of the end of the world. Wade didn't like to think about being part of the end of something; he wanted to be part of its beginning.

But Arin might have been right. Whether the world ended because of radiation sickness or because Tyran blew it up with an atomic bomb, it was still the end. And Wade had played his part in it. His efforts to undo the damage were worthless as long as he was trapped in the tower. Who else could do it? Tyran didn't care as long as he had his position of power. Dr. Lyst wasn't around.

Oh, if only I could get out of here! he thought. *I could still save the day.*

He frowned to himself. Save the day? How could he save anything when there was no one there to save *him?*

The guard returned at lunchtime with yet another tray of brown broth, bread, and water. He didn't speak to Wade at all, nor did he answer any of Wade's questions. He simply coughed and sneezed. His cheeks were flushed, and his eyes looked feverish. He left again.

Wade's mood shifted from anger to despair. He took to kicking at the door and screaming out of the arrow loop for someone to let him go. No one responded.

A siren sounded off and on throughout the afternoon, then went silent.

As night fell, Wade saw fires down in the city. When the guard eventually came late with the dinner tray, Wade asked about them.

"Funeral pyres," the man mumbled. "They're burning the dead."

He set the tray down on the table, and Wade saw that it held only a piece of bread and some water.

"The cook is out sick," the guard coughed. His speech was slurred, and his movements were slow and weak, as if he might collapse at any moment. Wade secretly wished he would. He also wondered if the guard could catch him if he ran for the door.

The guard grumbled to himself, then staggered toward the door before Wade could make up his mind. After going out, he closed and locked it.

In a furious burst of energy, Wade threw himself against the door and screamed, "Let me out of here!" His tantrum lasted a full 15 minutes, after which he felt drained and depressed. He cried himself to sleep.

That night he dreamed about Movan, lying in that dark room in the alleyway, his nose and eyes covered with yellow muck. He reached out for Wade and asked him in a raspy death rattle to take him to Arin's compound. "I've realized the error of my ways," Movan said. "Take me to Arin, where I'll be safe again."

Wade picked Movan up—in the dream he was no larger than a small boy—and carried him to the gates of Arin's compound. The gates were torn from their hinges. Arin's house was ransacked. The once-beautiful compound was desolate and scorched, as if an atomic blast had blown it away.

Still carrying Movan, Wade rushed to the shelter. The door was sealed shut. Wade put Movan down and pounded on the door for Arin to let them in. No one answered. Exhausted, Wade turned to Movan to apologize for his failure. Movan was now nothing more than a skeleton with a mustache above its upper teeth. It leered at him. Wade tried to step away, but the skeleton had hold of his ankle and wouldn't let go. Wade kicked at it, screaming again and again, "Get off! Get off!" He finally gave the skeleton the hardest kick he could manage, and it shattered into hundreds of pieces.

Wade went back to the shelter door and banged at it with his fists. "Please let me in!" he cried. "I'm sorry! I was wrong! I repent! I repent!"

When Wade woke up, he was standing at his cell door. His hands and arms were bruised. He'd been pounding at it in his sleep.

He slumped to the floor and wept until he ran out of tears. He thought of the Unseen One. "If You're the same as the God in my world," he heard himself praying, "then wake me up from this nightmare. Take me back to my coal cellar. I'm sorry for what I've done. Please ... save me!" He sobbed again, "Save me."

The guard didn't come the next morning. Wade tried to convince himself that the guard had simply forgotten about him. It was a mistake. He had no reason to worry.

When the guard didn't come for lunch, Wade grew anxious. Surely they had replacement guards. If his regular guard was sick, they'd send someone else.

Wade watched the city from the arrow loop. Except for the occasional car or man or woman rushing down the street, it seemed unnaturally quiet. A few times he thought he heard what sounded like rioting or looting, but the buildings blocked his view. Smoke from various fires rose continuously until a dull, brown haze hung over the city like an old ghost.

He paced from the door to the arrow loop and back again. His stomach ached from hunger. He prayed again to the

Unseen One for help, but he also started to give up believing it would come.

The city was dying, he knew. The end had arrived, just as Arin had always said. And Wade was doomed to watch it all from the window of a tower, where he, too, would die.

CHAPTER SIXTEEN

―❖―――――❖―

It was another dream, Wade thought. Dr. Lyst, gaunt and dying, had him by the shoulders and was shaking him.

"Get up," the doctor rasped at him, then coughed.

Wade winced as spittle hit his cheek.

It wasn't a dream. Dr. Lyst was leaning over him, a gray morning light on the walls behind him.

"Doctor?" Wade said, sitting up.

The doctor braced himself against the table. "I thought you were dead," he wheezed.

"I thought I was dreaming," Wade replied.

The doctor went into a coughing fit. It sounded as if every ounce of liquid in his lungs was coming up. When he finished, he said, "Tyran is dead."

Wade was speechless.

"He came down with the sickness. It seemed to attack him more quickly than some of us. I don't know how it is I'm still alive. But last night, right before he died, he muttered something about you being locked up here. I was too weak to find the keys. But I felt a little stronger this morning and … came … up …" He coughed again, then collapsed on the floor next to the table.

"Thank you," Wade said. "Thank you, thank you. I didn't know how I was going to get out."

"Help me back down the stairs," the doctor instructed. "I don't want to die up here either."

The journey was slow and difficult, but they eventually made it down the tower stairs. Dr. Lyst fell into the first chair they found in the hallway at the bottom.

"The old fox tricked me," Dr. Lyst explained. "As soon as I agreed to meet you at the Dome, he cornered me. I think he had a listening device on my communicator. Anyway, we argued, I told him what I really thought, and he put me under guard in my laboratory."

"He sent his guards to capture me."

"I'm sorry. I should have known better. Arin would've taken care of you."

"I came back to see you," Wade said. "I figured out why everyone was getting sick, and I thought we could stop it."

Dr. Lyst smiled weakly. "You were born to be a scientist," he said fondly. "Always thinking. Always speculating. I used my time under lock and key to investigate this illness. I was my own patient, you see. My notes are in the lab. You should read them." He went into another coughing fit. Then, recovering a little, he continued, "It's too late now. I'm dying. We're all dying."

Wade knelt next to the doctor. "Maybe not. By finding the source of the radiation leak—the viranium—we could seal it up."

The doctor looked at Wade with bloodshot eyes and slowly shook his head. "No," he said, then coughed again. "Take me back to the cot in my lab. I don't want to die in this hallway."

"You're not going to die."

The doctor grunted, then stretched out a hand for Wade's help. Again, slowly, they made their way to the lab. The halls were empty. The castle was silent. Wade suspected they were the only two living people inside.

Wade helped the doctor lie down on a cot near the lab table. The man didn't speak but breathed heavily and coughed occasionally. Wade thought he'd fallen asleep.

Unsure of what to do next, Wade went over to the desk and found a leather-bound book, the doctor's journal. The notes were scrawled in an almost illegible way. He scanned the pages and stopped at an entry from a couple of days before where the doctor had tersely described the symptoms of the illness.

"The timetable seems to vary from person to person," the doctor had written. "But the symptoms are nearly the same. In the first 48-72 hours, coldlike symptoms: runny nose, congestion, sore throat. All symptoms intensify over the next 24 hours or so, including a high fever. Gradual breakdown of the immune system."

A few pages held notations that Wade couldn't figure out. Then he found an entry that said, "Investigated viranium poisoning as possibility. All containers sealed. No leakage. No exposure. I have one more theory—"

"Wade," the doctor called from the cot.

Wade went over to him. "Yes, doctor?"

"Go to Arin."

"Now?"

"Yes."

"But what about you?"

"I'm dying."

"Come to Arin with me."

"No. I won't survive the journey. I'm very nearly dead now."

"You won't die."

Dr. Lyst chuckled. "It can't be helped. There's no cure."

"I don't understand," Wade said, his eyes brimming with tears. "You said in your journal that it wasn't the viranium. It wasn't poison from radioactivity."

"It wasn't."

"Then what is it? Where did this sickness come from?"

"Dear boy," the doctor said, then coughed. "It came from you."

A terrible burning worked its way through every ounce of Wade's body. "What?" he whispered.

"You are the host of this illness," Dr. Lyst said. "You brought this plague to us."

"No. No!" Wade cried.

Dr. Lyst closed his eyes. "Do you remember how I did a physical on you that first day you came here? I did blood tests then, remember?"

"I remember."

"You said you had just recovered from a flu, and I didn't know what that was. Well, after exhausting every other theory about this sickness, I studied your tests. Then I studied the samples of my own blood. There it was. Your flu is the thing that's killing us."

"But it was only a small flu," Wade protested. "It wasn't anything serious."

"It wasn't serious in your world. But in this world, which hasn't seen anything like it, it's fatal. Our immune systems don't work against it because it's completely new to us."

Wade put his head down, feeling overwhelmed by the truth.

Dr. Lyst stroked his hair gently. "There, there," he comforted. "It's not your fault. How could you know?"

"But … I caused this," Wade said into his lap. "Everyone is dying because of me."

Dr. Lyst wheezed for a moment, then said, "Or maybe Arin was right. It is the judgment of the Unseen One on all of us. You were simply His final sign, as Arin said. You were the means through which the Unseen One judged us."

Wade looked up at Dr. Lyst's face.

The doctor attempted to smile. "Terribly unscientific to say so, I know. But I'm dying now, and it doesn't matter anymore. Now, be a good boy and hand me that controller on the table."

The controller was a small device with a dozen electronic buttons on it. "What is it?" Wade asked as he placed it in the doctor's hand.

"My final gesture," he replied. "I've always had a backup plan in case things didn't go the way I thought they should. I'm going to blow this place to smithereens."

Wade gasped out, "You can't!"

Dr. Lyst worked his lips into a smile again. "Yes, I can. Do you think I want anyone in the future to learn my terrible secrets? Let *them* figure it out if they're so determined to blow each other up."

"But Doctor—"

"Go quickly to Arin, Wade. I'll make sure you're safely away before I push the button."

"But I don't want to leave you here!"

"Now is not the time to be sentimental. You always hoped to go back to your world anyway. You would have said good-bye to me then. Say good-bye now and be done with it."

Wade fought back the tears. "Good-bye."

"Hurry. And don't dilly-dally."

Wade ran out of the room without looking back.

CHAPTER SEVENTEEN

❖————————❖

Wade had the presence of mind to grab some fruit from a bowl on his way out of the castle. He ate it as he ran through the courtyard, across the bridge, then down the winding drive. He didn't know how long Dr. Lyst would give him before pushing the button, but he didn't want to take any chances.

At the bottom of the drive, Wade encountered a figure lying prone in the street. He went up to it to see if he could help. As he got closer, he saw it was a woman. The dead, staring eyes told him there wasn't a thing he could do.

Hers was the first of many bodies he saw as he raced blindly through the streets, hoping he was going toward Arin's compound. Not only were the people dying, but the animals had collapsed as well. Birds fell from the trees and struggled against their illness with flapping wings. Bloated horses lay dead along the streets. Dogs whimpered, then expired. Dead cats dotted the sidewalks.

Wade passed one shop where feverish looters tried to drag out merchandise. What was the point? he wondered. Or was it that the old habits refused to yield to the dying souls?

"It's the boy!" a man shouted.

Wade suddenly realized he'd forgotten to cover his head.

"He's the cause of all this!" a woman yelled. A small band of men and women headed for him. They stumbled weakly, like puppets held up by only half their strings.

"Stop!" another man shouted.

Wade dashed away and down an alley. He easily outran them.

Fires poured out of some of the shops and buildings. The streets were covered with broken glass, debris, and the occasional corpse. Wade tried not to look. The sight was too horrifying, particularly when he remembered he was the cause. *This is all my fault,* he said to himself again and again.

An old man stumbled in front of him, lurching and reeling, grabbed for him, then collapsed onto the road. He gasped once, then twice, then breathed out long and hard until he breathed no more. Wade fell against a nearby wall and shoved his fist into his mouth to keep from screaming or throwing up—he didn't know which was more likely.

Regaining a little composure after a few moments, Wade pressed on. A few blocks down the road, a younger man in a black uniform—one of Tyran's guards—recognized Wade. He blew a whistle and was soon joined by three more guards. They took up the chase after Wade.

These four weren't so easily outrun. Wade ducked down various streets and alleys, but they cut him off. They knew their way around the city much better than he did. Finally he jumped through a doorway into a large building. It looked like a hotel. The guards followed him.

He ran up one flight of stairs, down a hall, then up another flight. Up and up he went with the guards always behind, always pushing him on. Spotting an open window at the end of the next hallway, he went to the ledge and saw a fire escape that would take him back down to the street. He climbed out onto it and began his descent.

When he had gotten halfway down, one of the guards spied him from a window he was passing, opened it quickly, and grabbed for him. Wade sidestepped the guard's hand, but in the process he stumbled and fell off the side of the railing. Clawing wildly at the air, he caught hold of a rung on the fire escape ladder. It came unhitched from its spring and shot out horizontally, carrying Wade with it. When it reached its full length, it stopped suddenly, then coasted down toward the ground. As soon as it seemed safe, Wade leaped off, regained his footing, then sprinted away without looking back.

As he rounded a corner, he was nabbed by the first guard who'd seen him. "I've got you now!" the man announced with a leer.

At that instant, an enormous explosion rocked the city. Dr. Lyst had pushed the button, Wade knew, and there would be little left of Tyran's castle. The force of the blast caused windows to shatter around them. The guard, wanting to protect himself from the debris, let go of Wade, who immediately dived under a nearby car. He heard something strike the guard, and the guard yelled in pain. Wade looked out from beneath the vehicle. The guard, now on his knees, blood pouring from the side of his head, shouted at Wade and then sputtered as he tried to blow his whistle. Wade turned away, crawled out from under the other side of the car, and took off at high speed, turning into the next alley he found.

This alley led to another main street. He had no idea where he was. He hesitated. Should he go left or right? The rush to get away from the guards had turned him all around.

Help me, he prayed, then ran to the right. After 50 yards or so, the street deposited him onto a large courtyard—and the Dome. He was relieved to see something he recognized. Up at the top of the stairs, looters were carrying works of art out of the museum. One said something about the "blond-haired boy," but Wade didn't stick around to hear any more. He thought he remembered how Arin had brought him to the Dome a few days before and headed in that direction.

Several minutes later, Wade approached the gates of Arin's

compound. They were torn off their hinges, just as Wade had dreamed in the tower. His heart sank. He hurried into the compound and over to the house. Also as in the dream, it was ransacked. Half of it was a charred ruin, with its black timbers thrusting this way and that. But, contrary to Wade's dream, the forest was still there.

Wade took the path that he knew led to the shelter.

Once in the thick of the forest, he slowed down and tried to catch his breath. He also wanted to be careful. Whoever had ransacked the house might still be nearby. He looked around and noticed that the trees looked grayer somehow, as if even they were ready to give up on life. The flowers had dropped their petals and withdrawn their scents. The whole garden now smelled of soot, smoke, and ash like the rest of the city. Arin's paradise looked like an old, decaying park.

Reaching the shelter, he went around to the door. It was scratched, scuffed, and dented as if people had tried to break it down. Wade wondered where the attackers were now. Had they given up and gone away?

What would Arin and his family think if Wade pounded on the door now? Would they dismiss him as just another crazed native?

He knocked on the door. His small fist made tiny taps against the large, steel structure. He knocked again, harder. Then harder still. Finally as hard as he could. Nothing stirred on the other side. He began banging more heartily, pretending he was playing some sort of game. When no one responded, he attacked the door out of fear that they might never open it to him.

He started to shout, but he quickly realized his voice would probably draw a mob or Tyran's guards, if any of them were left.

His pounding on the door got him nowhere, so at last he sat down and waited. Still nothing happened. The shelter showed no signs of life. He was locked out and completely alone.

He tried to decide what to do next. Should he leave? Perhaps. But where would he go? Soon he would be the only living boy in the city. If Arin were right, he might be the only living boy in the entire world. How long were Arin and his family planning to stay inside the shelter? Days? Years?

Then, like a seed of terror, a thought grew in his mind. What if Arin and the others *couldn't* let him in? What if they were afraid that they'd catch whatever sickness Wade was carrying? *They should be afraid*, Wade realized. *Why would they be immune to it?*

No, they *didn't dare* let Wade in.

He struggled with this thought and fell into a deep despondency. He could no longer imagine what to do or where to go. He wished he had stayed in the tower—that Dr. Lyst had never opened the door—and then he would have died without experiencing this hopelessness, this final consequence of the sickness he'd brought to this world.

I am totally and completely alone, he thought. *Even the Unseen One has probably deserted me and gone into the shelter. I deserve to die out here.*

With nothing else to do, he lay down in the dirt and curled up into a small ball.

CHAPTER EIGHTEEN

The nightmares came not long after he'd fallen asleep. Out of the darkness, the dead came to accuse him of killing them. Their faces were twisted into grotesque masks. Their accusing, skeletal fingers were draped with decaying skin. But Wade didn't run from them. He stood his ground and listened to their harsh, raspy voices that called him a murderer.

"You're right," he replied to them. "And now I'm suffering for what I've done. I'm alone in a dead world. Alone."

He heard the sound of a crypt opening, with rusty hinges and the smell of moss. Hands reached out for him, beckoning him into the casket. He closed his eyes. The hands wrapped around his arms and shoulders and pulled at him. He felt his body being swept away … caught like a dead fish on a wave … pulling him … pulling him …

And then he saw a bright light and heard the voice of Arin whispering for him to wake up.

Wade's heart jumped at the sound of the voice, but he didn't open his eyes. He feared that he would look up and see nothing more than the closed shelter door. He feared the hope that the voice kindled inside him. He couldn't bear to have it dashed.

"Are you playing a game with us, boy?" Arin whispered.

Wade slowly opened his eyes. Arin's face came fully into view. Wade reached up and touched his cheek, wanting to make sure he wasn't dreaming. The skin was real. Arin was real. Wade looked around and saw the faces of Muiraq, Oshan, Etham, Pool, Nacob, Riv, and Hesham gazing back at him with worried expressions. He was inside the shelter with them.

Arin smiled at him with relief. "We were worried about you, boy," he said.

Wade threw himself into Arin's arms and cried as he'd never cried before.

❦ ————————— ❦

"We thought we heard someone knocking, but we didn't want to open the door until we were sure it wasn't a trick," Arin explained to Wade. They were all sitting around a large, metal table in what they called the "dining room" of the shelter. In the distance, Wade heard the lowing of cattle, the occasional bleating of sheep, and the chirping of many kinds of birds.

"We waited until night fell and then opened the door," Muiraq continued. "There you were, all curled up, sleeping so deeply. We pulled you in as quickly as we could and then closed the door again."

"The door is sealed tight from now on," Arin said. "You are the last to join us, and only because the Unseen One made it clear to me that you were allowed."

Wade hung his head low. "I don't deserve to be here," he said solemnly. "Why did the Unseen One tell you to let me in?"

"Because of your heart," Arin replied.

"What about it?"

"Did you not pray to the Unseen One and ask for His forgiveness? Didn't you ask Him to help you?"

Wade remembered his time in the tower. "Yes, I did."

"It was more than anyone else in this world did," Arin said gravely. "So He opened the door to you."

"But how did *you* know that?" Wade asked, mystified once again.

Arin shrugged.

"What will happen to the world now?"

"For 40 days and nights, it will go through a terrible upheaval. All living things will die—not only people, but the animals and plants as well. The world will drown in the illness you brought."

"The illness *I* brought," Wade said softly.

"Everything that humanity has trusted in until now will be obliterated: its technology, its knowledge, its lies. After 40 days, my family and I will rise up from the shelter to begin anew. The Unseen One will start pure again what had been corrupted."

Wade looked puzzled, then asked, "But why aren't you sick? Why didn't you catch the disease I brought? You should be afraid now."

"I told you when you arrived that the Unseen One would protect us. And He has, us and all the animals and other living things here. Whatever illness you brought simply hasn't affected us."

Muiraq stood up. "This is enough talk for now," she announced. "There are chores to do, and then we must eat our dinner. Go on now!" She shooed them all away as if they were birds on a fence.

Later, when Wade was standing near one of the large aquariums, watching the saltwater fish gliding around carelessly, Arin approached him.

"You have something on your mind," Arin said.

Wade almost asked him how he knew, but he decided it was a mystery he would never understand. So he said directly, "I feel terrible about what happened. I'm responsible for this catastrophe."

"In what way?" Arin asked.

"I came here and introduced terrible bombs, and worse, I spread a sickness that"—it seemed incredible, but he said it anyway—"that killed everyone. If I hadn't come, then ..." He paused and gently bit his lower lip. He was tired of crying and didn't want to start again.

"There now, stay strong," Arin said warmly. "Let's try to untangle this mess you're in."

"How?"

"Well, the first thing you should remember is that you didn't come here on your own. I believe the Unseen One brought you here for a purpose."

Wade thought about it for a moment. It was true that he hadn't asked—or done anything—to come to this world. One minute he was in his coal cellar, and the next minute he was here. "That's right," he agreed. "But my purpose was to bring sickness and death."

"Sickness and death, yes. Just as at another time you could have come and brought life and light to our world. But you didn't. The Unseen One brought you here to convey His justice to an evil world that demanded it." Arin picked up a broom and leaned on the handle as though it were a staff. "Sooner or later the Unseen One's promises are always fulfilled, you see. You happened to be the way He fulfilled this promise."

"It's still a terrible promise to fulfill."

"I agree," he said. "And I don't suppose you have to like it any more than I liked preaching a message of doom for so many years. Do you think I enjoyed that? I was cut off from my relatives, ostracized by my neighbors, ridiculed in my community. When they weren't laughing at me, they were cursing me. But that's the nature of things in this world. The truth will always set us apart. Sometimes that truth soothes and heals, and sometimes it cuts to the marrow. As a result, our service to the Unseen One will always put us at odds with unbelievers. But we have to take our part and do what He wants us to do."

"But if I hadn't come …"

Arin looked at Wade like a disapproving teacher. "That's a useless question, now, isn't it? Granted, you did some foolish things once you got here. But those things played themselves out as they should have. You allowed wicked men to deceive you, and they ultimately paid the price for it."

Wade considered that notion. "What price did *I* pay for what I did?" he asked.

"What price do you *think* you should have paid?"

"I don't know."

"More?" Arin stroked his chin in consideration. "Well, now, I believe you've suffered as much as you needed to suffer to realize your foolishness. You saw where you went wrong, and you asked the Unseen One to forgive you."

"Yes."

"Then what else is there to be said? What else is there to be paid?"

Wade struggled to understand what Arin was saying.

Arin put his arm around Wade's shoulders, and they began to walk. "I know how you feel, Wade," Arin said softly. "Deep in your heart, you feel guilty because you're in this shelter and you don't think you deserve to be. Am I on the right track?"

Wade nodded.

"You think that maybe if you suffered *more*, you might feel less guilty. Is that the idea?

Wade didn't reply, but he knew it was so.

"Then listen to me and listen closely," Arin went on. "There's no amount of suffering you can do to deserve the love of the Unseen One. He saved you because of your *repentant heart*—because you realized there was nothing more you could do. You had to give up and ask for His help. That's as much as any of us can do. The truth of the matter is that none of us deserve to be saved. We should all be outside, dying with the rest."

"But you're all so good and wise and—"

"Don't be ridiculous!" Arin corrected him. "We're men and women, flesh and blood, as prone to disobedience as anyone. The only thing we did was to listen to the Unseen One when no one else would."

Wade didn't know what to say.

Arin smiled. "You think about it for a while. Maybe it'll make sense one day. Meanwhile . . ." Arin handed Wade a feed pouch. "I want you to go over and see that the horses get their dinner. You can start with Bethel. The feed is in that long box against the wall."

Wade looked at Arin curiously. It seemed like a strange turn to their conversation.

"Go on," Arin said. "Just put the pouch over her mouth and the strap over the top of her head. But be careful. She *does* bite." In the dim light, Wade thought Arin looked a little sad, but he couldn't imagine why.

Wade went over to the feed box and filled the pouch with oats. He then went to Bethel's stall, hesitating at the door.

Arin was still watching him. "Go on," he said again.

Wade shrugged and stepped into the stall. It was dark. "Bethel?" he called out. He spotted her toward the rear. He approached her slowly so as not to scare her, then put the feed pouch up to her mouth. She began to eat. He then reached up to put the strap over the top of her head. "There you go," he said and turned back to the door.

Something crunched under his feet.

"What is that?" he asked and lifted his foot to look. He lost his balance and fell over on his side. Embarrassed, he laughed to himself and said, "You're such a clumsy oaf."

"What did you say?" a woman asked.

Wade replied, "I said I'm such a clumsy oaf." And then he realized that the woman was his mother and he wasn't in the stable with Bethel at all. He was lying in his bed—his *own* bed—in his own home in his own world.

CHAPTER NINETEEN

❖

Wade looked at his mother, his face wide open with surprise. "Mom?" he said.

Her eyes were moist. She'd been crying. "Hello, son," she replied.

"What happened?" he croaked and started to sit up. He felt too weak, though, and decided to stay where he was.

"You've had a terrible relapse," she answered. "A high fever. I was worried sick. I knew I shouldn't have let you out of bed. You never should have been down in the coal cellar."

"How long?" His throat was dry; he was dying of thirst.

"Since this morning," she replied. "I got the telegram and went down to tell you about it, but you were unconscious in the coal cellar. The doctor said you must have fainted from trying to fill the bucket." She began to cry again. "I shouldn't have let you do that."

Wade patted his mother's hand. "It's okay, Mom. I feel a little weak, but I'm all right. I had the strangest dream, though."

"You rest while I get you some soup. Then you can tell me all about it." She dabbed her eyes with a tissue, then walked to the door.

Wade suddenly realized something she'd said. "Mom—"

"Yes, son?"

"What telegram? Is there news about Dad?"

She reached into her pocket and pulled out the folded, yellow sheet of paper. "There's news," she said and started to cry all over again.

Wade held his breath.

She composed herself and continued, "Your father is alive and well, Wade! He had to parachute out of his plane and wound up breaking his leg in the jungle, miles and miles from anywhere. Some island natives have been sheltering him until they could find help. Isn't that wonderful?"

Relief washed over him. "Yeah, it's great."

She came back over to the bed and hugged her son tight, then made a fuss for crying so much and went out to make him some soup.

"Sheltered," he said softly to himself and stretched long and hard. "What a dream!"

Only after he'd finished his soup did he remember the top-secret atomic bomb plans. He searched his robe and under his pajamas, then noticed that he was wearing a different pair. His mother had changed his clothes.

"You had coal dust all over your other pair of pajamas," she said when he asked her about it. "And they were soaking wet from your fever."

"What did you do with the papers I had?" he asked hesitantly.

"What papers?"

"I had some papers tucked under my pajama top, with drawings and a lot of writing."

"You didn't have any papers," she said.

"How about down in the coal cellar?" he persisted.

She looked at him impatiently. "You didn't have any papers, I'm telling you. I would have seen them. Were they school papers?"

"No."

"Then you must have left them somewhere else, because they're not around here."

Suddenly he remembered the exact moment when he had handed them over to Dr. Lyst.

And he wondered.

"Well?" Jack asked when he phoned Whit after reading the manuscript the next day.

"It's a remarkable story," said Whit.

"I thought so, too."

"It has a familiar ring to it, like the previous one."

"I don't suppose there's any point in asking if you think it's true or not," Jack said.

"At least this time we have those newspaper clippings—and a full name."

"Wade Mullens," Jack said, then asked, "Did you go to the library?"

"Uh huh."

"What did you find?"

Jack could hear the rustling of papers as Whit looked over the copies he'd made. "I found the original articles from the *Odyssey Times,* the ones that were shoved into the manuscript. I also found a follow-up article about Ronald Mullens."

"That's the father?"

"Yes. The article told all about his extraordinary adventures in the Pacific."

"That part is true?"

"It's amazing," Whit said. "His plane was shot down, so he had to parachute into the jungle. He broke his leg after hitting a tree and was nursed back to health by the natives—who also kept him hidden from the Japanese. They didn't even realize the war was over until three weeks after it ended." Whit paused, then said for emphasis, "They built him a shelter, Jack."

Jack hummed thoughtfully. "A shelter. You think there's a connection?"

"You should read the article," Whit said. "I have it here."

"Okay."

"The final quote from Wade Mullens is interesting."

"What did he say?"

Whit picked up the article. "He said he was glad to have his father home and that it was only by the grace of the Unseen One that it was possible."

"He *said* that?" Jack asked. "He used the phrase 'Unseen One'?"

"That's what he said. The reporter then asked him what an Unseen One was."

"What did Wade say?"

"Wade said, and I quote, 'It's God, of course.'"

Jack was quiet for a moment. Both men were thinking the same thing. "Whit," Jack finally said, "can we find out any more about the Mullens family? Are they still in Odyssey? If not, where did they go from here? I think we need to do a little detective work on this."

"I was hoping you'd think so," Whit replied, pleased.

"Shall we check the city hall records?"

"I'll drive over and pick you up."

And now, a preview of the exciting *Passages*, Book 3!

CHAPTER ONE

◆————————◆

"Ready or not, here I come!" a child's voice called out from somewhere behind the shed.

Madina Nicholaivitch giggled and scrambled to find a hiding place. She'd already hidden once behind the well and once in the garage, and now she had to think of somewhere little Johnny Ziegler wouldn't think to find her.

Johnny shouted, excitement in his voice, "I'm coming, Maddy!"

Everyone called her Maddy now except her grandparents, who still spoke in Russian and called her Dreamy Madina in that tongue. It didn't matter to them that they'd been living in America, this town of Odyssey, for 10 years now. "We will not forsake our traditions, no matter where we live," Grandma had said.

On the other hand, Maddy's father, Boris, now refused to speak any Russian. He said he was protesting the Russian Revolution of 1917 that drove them, persecuted and destitute, from their home in St. Petersburg. "We're in America now," he stated again and again in his clipped English. "We must speak as Americans."

"The revolution will not last," Maddy's Grandpa proclaimed several times a year, especially in October, on the anniversary of the revolution.

"It is now 1927, is it not?" Maddy's father argued. "They have killed the czar, they have destroyed everything we once held dear, and they are closing our churches. I turn my back on Russia as Russia turned its back on us. We are Americans now."

So Madina became Maddy and spoke American because she was only two when they came to America. She never really learned Russian anyway, except for odd phrases from her grandparents. Refugees that they were, they'd started off in New York and drifted west to Chicago as opportunities from various friends and relatives presented themselves. Boris had been an accomplished tailor back in St. Petersburg, so his skill was in demand wherever they went. Then they'd heard from a cousin who owned a tailor shop in the small town of Odyssey and wanted Boris to join him in the business. They called the firm Nichols Tailor & Clothes, Nichols being the English corruption of their original Russian name, and made clothes for nearly everyone, including the mayor of Odyssey.

Maddy was unaffected by all the changes and upheaval in their lives. She seemed contented and happy regardless of where they were. The world could have been falling apart around her and she would have carried on in her pleasant, dreamlike way, lost in fantasies like *Alice in Wonderland*, *Peter Pan*, and the many other stories she read at the local library.

She often pretended to be a girl with magical powers in a fairy-tale world. Or she played out a dream she'd been having night after night for the past two weeks. In the dream, she was a lady-in-waiting to a princess with raven black hair and the most beautiful face Maddy had ever seen.

"You must come and help me," the princess said to her every night in the dream.

"I will," Maddy replied. And then she would wake up.

She had told her mother about the dream. But her mother smiled indulgently and dismissed it as she had most of Maddy's fanciful ideas.

Apart from pretending to be in fairy tales, Maddy enjoyed playing games like hide-and-seek with the smaller neighborhood children. Her mother often said that she would be a teacher when she grew up because she loved books and children so much.

Maddy circled their old farm-style house that had been built with several other similar houses on the edge of town. It had gray shingles, off-white shutters, and a long porch along the front. She ducked under the clothesline that stretched from the porch post to a nearby pole. The shirts and underclothes brushed comfortingly against her face, warmed by the sun. She then spied a small break in the trelliswork that encased the underside of the porch. That would be her hiding place, she decided—under the porch.

She pressed a hand down on her thick, curly, brown hair to keep it from getting caught on any of the trellis splinters and went only as far under as she dared, to the edge of the shadows. The dirt under her hands and bare legs was cold. She tried not to get any of it on her dark blue peasant dress, which her father had made especially for her. She could smell the damp earth and old wood from the porch. In another part of the garden, she heard her little brother squeal with delight as their mother played with him in the late-summer warmth.

"I'm going to find you," little Johnny, the boy from next door, called out.

Maddy held her breath as she saw his legs appear through the diamond shapes of the trellis. He hesitated, but the position of his feet told her that he had his back to the porch. Maybe he wouldn't see the gap she'd crawled through. He moved farther along, getting closer to the gap, so she moved farther back into the shadows and darkness. The hair on her neck bristled. She'd always worried that a wild animal might have gone under the porch to live, just as their dog Babushka had when she'd given birth to seven puppies last year. But

Maddy's desire to keep Johnny from finding her was greater than her fear, so she went farther back and farther in.

The porch, like a large mouth, seemed to swallow her in darkness. The trelliswork, the sunlight, and even Johnny's legs, now moving to and fro along the porch, faded away as if she'd slowly closed her eyes. But she knew she hadn't. She held her hand up in front of her face and wiggled her fingers. She could see still them.

Then, from somewhere behind her, a light grew, like the rising of a sun. But it wasn't yellow like dawn sunlight; it was white and bright, like the sun at noon. She turned to see, wondering where the light had come from. She knew well that there couldn't be a light farther under the porch, that she would soon reach a dead end at the cement wall of the basement.

As she looked at the light, she began to hear noises as well. At first they were indistinct, but then she recognized them as the sounds of people talking and moving. Maddy wondered if friends from town had come to visit. But the voices were too numerous for a small group of friends. This sounded more like a big crowd. And mixed with the voices were the distinct sounds of horses whinnying and the clip-clop of their hooves and the grating of wagon wheels on a stony street.

Crawling crablike and being careful not to bump her head on the underside of the porch, Maddy moved in the direction of the light and sounds. The noises grew louder, and, once she squinted a little, she could see human and horse legs moving back and forth, plus the distinct outline of wagon wheels.

It's a busy street, she thought, but then she reminded herself, *There's no busy street near our house.* The sight inflamed her imagination, and she ventured still closer and closer to the scene. *It's like crawling out of a small cave,* she thought. Then her mind raced to the many stories she'd read about children who had stepped through a hole or mirror or doorway and wound up in a magical land. Her heart beat excitedly as she thought—*hoped*—that maybe it was about to happen to her. Perhaps she would get to see something wondrous; perhaps she was going to enter a fairy tale.

At the edge of the darkness, she glanced up and realized she was no longer under the porch. The coarse planks of plywood and the two wheels directly in front of her and two wheels directly behind her made her think she must be under a wagon. More startling was that the porch, the trellis, Johnny, and even her house had disappeared.

A man shouted, "Yah!" and snapped leather reins, and the wagon moved away from her. She stayed still, afraid she might get caught under the wheels, but they didn't touch her. In a moment she was crouched in an open space, sunlight pouring down onto her. People were crowded around, and she stood up with embarrassment on her face, certain they were wondering who she was and where she'd come from.

A man grabbed her arm and pulled her quickly into the crowd. "You'd better get out of the road, little lady," he warned. "Do you want to get run over by the procession?"

Besides that, no one seemed to notice her. But she noticed them. Her eyes were dazzled by the bright colors of the hundreds—maybe even thousands—of people lined up on both sides of the avenue. Trees sprung out from among them like green fountains. Tall buildings stood behind them with enormous columns and grand archways. Maddy blinked again. The colors seemed too bright somehow, much richer than the colors she was used to seeing. Then she smiled to herself: They looked just like the colors in so many of the illustrated stories she'd read.

She noticed that some of the people clutched flags and

banners, while others held odd-looking, rectangular-shaped hats to their chests, and a few carried children up on their shoulders. What struck Maddy most were the peculiar garments everyone wore. The women were in long, frilly dresses, not unlike Maddy's own peasant dress but far more intricate in their design, billowing out at the waist like tents. The men had on long coats and trousers that only went to just below their knees. The rest of their legs were covered with white stockings. On their feet they wore leather shoes with large, square buckles. The men had ponytails, she noticed, and hats that came to three-pointed corners.

The scene reminded her of the last Fourth of July, when she had stood along Main Street with the rest of Odyssey for the big parade, followed by fireworks and picnic food in the park. Some of the people in that parade had dressed the same as the people she saw now. It was the style of clothes worn when America won its independence.

Unlike the parade in Odyssey, however, this parade didn't seem very happy. Most of the people stood with stern expressions on their faces. A few looked grieved. Several women wiped tears from their eyes. Maddy suspected she had formed the wrong impression of what she was seeing. Maybe it wasn't a parade; maybe it was a funeral procession.

"Did someone die?" Maddy asked the man who'd pulled her from the street.

He gazed at her thoughtfully and replied, "Our nation, little lady. Our nation."

A regiment of soldiers now marched down the avenue. The men were dressed in the same outfits as those in the crowd, but all were a solid blue color, and they had helmets on their heads and spears or swords in their hands. They broke their ranks and spread out to the edge of the crowd.

"The king is coming, and we want you to be excited about it," one of them said gruffly.

"He's not *our* king!" someone shouted from the thick of the crowd.

The soldier held up his sword menacingly. "You can be excited or arrested," he threatened. "The choice is yours."

The soldiers moved off to stir up other parts of the crowd. Across the avenue, a fight broke out, and Maddy watched in horror as three soldiers began to beat and kick a man they'd knocked down. They dragged him away while the rest of the soldiers stood with their swords and spears at the ready.

What kind of parade is this, she wondered, *where the people are forced to enjoy it or be beaten?* As if to answer her question, Maddy remembered the stories her father told of the Russian revolutionaries who demanded that people parade and salute even when they didn't want to.

Halfhearted cheers worked their way through the crowd as a parade of horses approached and passed, soldiers sitting erect on their backs, swords held high in a formal salute. Then a large band of musicians with woodwinds and brass instruments came by, playing a lively song of celebration. Next came several black, open-topped carriages, each with people dressed in colorful outfits of gold and silver that twinkled in the sunlight. The men wore white shirts with lacy collars. The women wore hats with brightly colored feathers sticking out of the backs. They waved and smiled at the crowd.

Maddy noticed one man in particular who seemed almost as unhappy as some of the people in the crowd. He had a pockmarked face, unfriendly eyes, a narrow nose, and thinning, wiry hair. Unlike the rest of the parade, he didn't wear a colorful jacket but one of solid black—as if he, too, were mourning something. Occasionally he lifted his hand in a wave, but

Maddy was struck by the look of boredom on his face. It seemed to require considerable effort for him to be pleasant to the crowd.

At the end of this particular procession came the largest carriage of all. Gold on the outside, its seats were made of a plush, red material. A man sat alone on the rear seat—propped up somehow to raise him higher than he normally would have been—and waved happily at the crowds. He was a pleasant-looking, middle-aged man with ruddy cheeks, big eyes, and wild, curly hair.

"I was wondering if he'd wear that stupid wig," someone muttered nearby.

"It's no worse than that coat," someone else commented.

The man's coat displayed the colors of the rainbow and had large buttons on the front. Maddy smiled. It made him look a little like a clown.

"I can't bear it," a woman cried as large tears streamed down her face. Even with the tears, she waved a small flag back and forth.

"What's wrong?" Maddy asked the woman. "Why are you crying?"

The woman dabbed at her face with a handkerchief. "Because it's the end of us all," she replied with a sniffle.

"Aye," an elderly man behind her agreed. "When the barbarians parade down the streets of Sarum, it's the end of Marus."

Suddenly a group of soldiers who had been following the golden carriage with muskets slung over their shoulders spread out to the crowds, thrusting flags and banners into their hands. "Take these and follow us to the palace," they commanded.

"Only after I've had my brain replaced with a beetroot," the elderly man said defiantly.

A soldier hit him in the stomach with the butt of his musket. The man doubled over in pain. "You'll follow no matter what kind of brain you have!" the soldier growled.

"Leave us alone!" a woman shouted. "Why don't you go back to Palatia where you belong?"

"And deprive our king of his spoils?" another soldier called back. "That wouldn't do."

The man who'd been hit recovered his breath, grumbled something Maddy didn't understand, then stepped out onto the avenue to follow the soldiers. Maddy was swept along with him and the rest of the crowd around her. Before she knew it, the man's flag—a small, rectangular cloth of red with a single star in the middle—was in her hand. He smiled at her. "You'll enjoy waving it more than I will," he suggested with a pained expression on his face. Eventually, she lost him in the crowd.

Worried that she might get in trouble, Maddy held the flag up and swung it as she walked. It didn't occur to her that she had no idea where she was or if she could find her way back to her porch. If this was a dream she was having or, better still, a magical place she'd found like Alice in Wonderland, she was curious to see what would happen next. "Dreamy Madina" was like that. But she wasn't too pleased about the nasty soldiers or the unhappiness of the people.

Maddy followed the crowd up the avenue until it joined yet another broad street. They seemed to walk for miles. Because she was surrounded on all sides by the crowd, she couldn't see much of the city. Only occasionally did a large building poke skyward beyond someone's head or shoulder. She wished she could stop to look longer at the great pillars and round towers or to read the names on the statues of men in brave and noble postures. Otherwise, she caught only glimpses of shops and homes made of brick and stone.

Just as Maddy's legs started to ache from the long walk, the crowd slowed to a halt. Then, after a moment, it slowly moved forward again, now through a large gate made of wrought iron and gold posts. She found herself in a parklike area with level grounds and manicured grass. A single driveway curved around in a half-moon shape and stopped at the double front doors of a palace. At least Maddy assumed it was a palace, for she'd never seen such a majestic building in her life.

The front door stood at the center of two wings, made of yellow stone, that spread out to the left and the right. There were three stories, each with rows of tall windows that reflected the day like jewels. Maddy's eye was drawn to a gold rotunda over the center section, where the front doors were. On top of the rotunda was a statue of something that looked to her like an angel.

The crowd was instructed by the soldiers to sit down on the grass. The man in the golden carriage stood up to address the throng. His voice was deep and booming but still hard to hear since he was some distance away.

"I, King Willem, declare a national holiday for my subjects, the people of Marus," he declared.

"We're not your subjects!" a man shouted from somewhere deep in the crowd. Soldiers instantly moved in to find the culprit.

The king ignored him. "Let this be a time of celebration!" he continued. "A time of feasts and banquets unlike anything seen in your lifetime!"

"As if I ever expected to see a *Palatian* king on the throne in my lifetime," an old man with a craggy face growled softly off to Maddy's right.

"Let the musicians make music, let sweet drinks flow, and let the food fill our bellies!" the king called out. "From this day forward, Palatia *and* Marus are intertwined, united by fate and by victory."

"It's *our* fate thanks to *his* victory," the same man muttered sarcastically.

The king continued, "And now I beseech every man, woman, and child to join me in celebrating my marriage to one of your own, the pure and gracious Annison!"

With this, a woman stepped out through one of the palace's front doors. Maddy gasped. The woman had raven black hair and a slender face, with a smile that seemed to light up everything around her. It was the most beautiful face Maddy had ever seen.

"It's the princess from my dream," she said out loud to a woman next to her.

The woman grunted and turned away.

Maddy craned her neck to see better. Annison wore a beautiful, red-velvet dress that highlighted the redness of her lips and the blush of her cheeks. She looked shy and slightly embarrassed to be standing in front of so many people. Lifting her hand, she gave an awkward wave.

Though it was a slight gesture, the crowd came alive now, with all the people leaping to their feet to cheer her. They cheered in a way they hadn't cheered for the king at any point in his procession—wildly and exuberantly. He didn't seem to mind, though. He stretched out his hand to her, his face filled with pride.

"I can't believe she's marrying him," a woman nearby sneered in the midst of the shouts and cheers. "She's a Marutian. She should be ashamed."

"She's an orphan girl," another woman said with a shrug. "Who knows what her lineage is? For all we know, she's a Palatian herself."

"She may be our only hope," an old man observed thoughtfully. The two women looked at him uncomfortably and shut up.

Maddy didn't understand what any of it meant. All she knew was that the princess of her dream was real in this strange world, and now she'd lost sight of her because of the crowd.

"You must come and help me," the princess had said in the dream.

And Maddy had promised she would. With that thought in mind, she pressed herself forward through the crowd. She was determined to get to the front door of the palace—and Annison.

FOCUS ON THE FAMILY ®

At Focus on the Family, we work to help you really get to know Jesus and equip you to change your world for Him.

We realize the struggles you face are different from your parents' or your little brother's, so we've developed a lot of resources specifically to help you live boldly for Christ, no matter what's happening in your life.

Besides exciting novels, we have Web sites, magazines, booklets, and devotionals . . . all dealing with the stuff you care about.

Focus on the Family Magazines

We know you want to stay up-to-date on the latest in your world — but it's hard to find information on entertainment, trends, and relevant issues that doesn't drag you down. It's even harder to find magazines that deliver what you want and need from a Christ-honoring perspective.

That's why we created *Breakaway* (for teen guys), *Brio* (for teen girls), and *Clubhouse* (for tweens, ages 8 to 12). So, don't be left out — sign up today!

Breakaway
Teen guys
breakawaymag.com

Brio
Teen girls
briomag.com

Clubhouse
Tweens ages 8 to 12
clubhousemagazine.com

Weekly Radio Show
whitsend.org

Phone toll free: (800) A-FAMILY (232-6459)

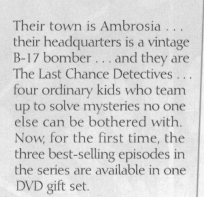